Anonymous

Little Blue-eyes

And other Field and Flower Stories

Anonymous

Little Blue-eyes
And other Field and Flower Stories

ISBN/EAN: 9783744750172

Printed in Europe, USA, Canada, Australia, Japan

Cover: Foto ©Andreas Hilbeck / pixelio.de

More available books at **www.hansebooks.com**

LITTLE BLUE-EYES,

AND

OTHER FIELD AND FLOWER STORIES.

BY THE

AUTHOR OF "MY YOUNG DAYS,"
"LITTLE LIVES," ETC.

WITH TWELVE ILLUSTRATIONS.

SEELEY, JACKSON, & HALLIDAY, 54, FLEET STREET,
LONDON. MDCCCLXXV.

CONTENTS.

———◆———

LIST OF ILLUSTRATIONS.

LITTLE BLUE-EYES DOWN THE LANE.

THE little Blue-eyes had a secret to keep. I mean those little Blue-eyes on the green bank which people call Speedwell—those beautiful little fellows that peep at you so cunningly as you pass from among the yellow buttercups, and the long weeds, and the twisting brambles underneath the hedge. They had a secret to keep. You would never have thought it. You would have felt sure that they had nothing in the world to trouble themselves about; but that from day-dawn to sunset they only had to shine out, and look pretty, and be as good-tempered as possible. This part of their duty they did to perfection certainly, and I fancy there were very few little flowers that held up their heads so well, or that kept themselves so clean and neat, and so far out of the dirt. And that, you know, is a duty. If other people, as well as the little Speedwells, kept a bright, happy face all the day long, it would be a good thing indeed. And I wish next time you go down the lane, you would just look at them, and see if I am not telling the truth. I know that if ever I feel sulky or out of sorts, a peep at the little Blue-eyes always does me good.

But I was going to tell you about the secret. Let me begin at the beginning. Very early in the morning the sun got up, for it was warm weather, and not the sort for anybody to stay in bed. The long grass was waking up, and the buttercups lifting up their heads to say good morning to their great warm friend in the blue sky. The daisies, too, were winking their little eyes as if they were only half awake. Then the Speedwells spread out their soft blue petals, wondering what this bright day would bring them.

It was just at that moment that little Jenny Wren flew out of her snug nest in the bank, and twittered the secret to them all as she passed.

" My babies are all out of the shell this morning, Blue-eyes ! Such little darlings they are ; oh, such little darlings. But don't you tell anybody, Blue-eyes, mind you don't tell ! "

And then she flew away, dear little Jenny did, as if she was glad to stretch her wings after such a long sitting still. And the Blue-eyes made up their minds that they wouldn't tell. No, not for anything ! It would have deen very nice just to turn their pretty eyes round and take a peep at the new babies. But they must not do that, for they had been put just in the right place, and it was their duty to look straight up at the sun, who is king of almost all the flowers, you know. So they would not turn round even to look at their own little charge.

They were very short, young flowers as yet, nestling among the grass; by and by, they would grow bigger, and taller, and bushier, and stretch out farther, but I don't think they would be so pretty then.

When the sun had got higher up in the sky, the blackbird came and sang to them, opening his beautiful yellow beak, and giving them the sweetest music. It was meant, I fancy, for his little love; but the Blue-eyes took it all to themselves, and it didn't matter much. And when he had done his song, he had his breakfast, and they watched him with a great deal of interest. I think it must have been as hard for the little flowers as for you and me to understand the pleasure of dragging up that long worm, snapping him in half, and swallowing him down. They had had their sweet draught of morning dew, and that seemed much nicer, and it made them feel so well and look so fresh! But then, again, we should not like a breakfast of morning dew; so, after all, I suppose, we must leave everyone to his own fancy.

When the blackbird had flown away, there came a number of little boys down the lane, all on their way to school, and the Speedwells watched them as they passed. I don't think the boys cared much about the flowers, yet as they came along they peered into the bank very closely. What were they looking for? I don't think our little friends would ever have guessed, if one small boy had not let it out. He was a little red-haired urchin, with a bright, round face, and eyes the very image of the little Speedwell.

" I'm sure there is a nest in here," he cried. " I say, you little blue things, isn't there now? "

But the little Blue-eyes would not tell. They were very speaking eyes, too; they seemed to have a world of fun in them, and a world of happiness beside. But they were not tell-tale eyes, not they! So the little boy went away, and Jenny Wren came back again, and settled down in her nest for a long time.

Then it grew very hot, and the ground got dry and hard, and the sun stared down into those little blue-eyed subjects of his, as if he would put them out of countenance. And, indeed, he did make them feel rather queer, and very much inclined to shrivel up all round and die. But still they looked up at him in their little innocent way, and never believed he could do them any harm. For he was their hero, you see. And yet, by and by, they were rather glad, I think, to see a great cloud come and cover up his face; and when the nice, cool drops of rain fell, they were gladder still. I dare say they thought it was the sun that melted the cloud for them, for they took a deep draught, and then they looked up in a very ecstacy of merry delight, as if they would cry out, " Oh, thanks, oh, thanks ! "

It was just then that a poor tired mother came with her little child, and sat down to rest on the cool bank under shelter from the rain. There was a great oak to shelter her, but it did not stretch out far enough to steal the rain-drops from the flowers. The little child saw them all covered with the bright drops, and he reached out his hand for them. " Yes, gather them, Johnny," said his mother, " they are nice home flowers, and they tell us we shall 'Speed well' and get home quick. And that's good news, Johnny, after all this long day's tramp."

And the boy gathered some of them in his little hand, and then they went away. But the Blue-eyes whispered to each other, as they parted, not to forget the secret.

By and by, when the sun had gone down, and it was a clear, cool evening, Jenny Wren flew out again to get a breath of air, before settling for the night, and again she whispered : "Don't tell, Blue-eyes, don't tell!" And the Blue-eyes nodded, for there was a gentle breeze blowing over the bank.

Only five minutes later, and the little red-haired boy came creeping along the lane.

This time we know what he was coming for, and the Speedwells might well keep their eyes wide open, and ruffle out their green leaves to cover up all spaces. He had a pinafore full of stones which he kept throwing, one at a time, into the hedge. " If only I can make the old birds fly out," he said, "I shall know where to find the nest." Wasn't it happy that Jenny had just gone out? Once, his rough, brown hand came diving in among the flowers, and one of our little friends was all crushed up, and never lifted its head any more. But the Blue-eyes did not tell; in fact, they looked supremely unconscious. And after peeping and peering about, at last the little boy went away. And then back came the mother-bird, chirruping her thanks. And very tired of their long day's watching, the Blue-eyes shut themselves up and went to sleep.

I have only told you about one day, but
you will easily fancy the rest; for all the
days are much alike to the happy flowers;
and those bright, sunny hours flew quickly
by.

It was just as the Blue-eyes had grown
tall and straggly, and were beginning to
think of dropping off their soft azure petals
—it was just then that the little wrens flew
out of the nest. It was a happy time for
Jenny; and indeed she might well be thank-
ful, for I could tell you stories of nest-rob-
bing all down that lane that would surprise
you. The wonder is that any little birds
ever live to grow up, but that is neither here
nor there.

The last thing, when all was done, and
Jenny had seen all her sons out in the world,
and had taken her last look at the empty
nest, just to make sure that nothing was left

behind—then she stopped a moment to thank her friends on the bank.

"You never told anybody, Blue-eyes! That was good of you! And now they are all off, and my mind is easy! Good-night, little Blue-eyes, good-night!"

And then there came a soft evening breeze, and it blew all the little blue petals away. They were willing enough to vanish, those little Blue-eyes, knowing that others would come after them, and that they should never be missed. There had been quite a little family of them, while the nest was full, and they had kept handing on the secret from one to another, as some died away and others were gathered. Now there was no message to hand on. "But we didn't tell," they murmured as they fell; "we never told!"

Good-night, little Blue-eyes, good-night!

II

THE FIR--CONE'S MISTAKE.

"Up here, right up here! Was there ever a jollier little fellow than I am!" cried a little green Fir-cone, and certainly, if a good position is a fine thing, he was about in the rights of it. For his tree was the topmost tree of the wood, and his wood went climbing up the mountain, and was ever so many hundred feet above the sea. Where the Fir-cone would have fallen to if some eagle had picked him off and let him drop, it makes one dizzy to think. The saucy little green Fir-cone. It was a kind of perpetual "I'm the king of the castle" with him from morning to night, and you know how that song provokes one to all kinds of mischief. Let me tell you a little bit of his way of talking, and you will see how nice, and delightful, and perfectly delicious it would have been to have knocked his head off. If only he had had a head; but as he hadn't, what could you do?

"I'm here, at the very tip-top, above you all, out of sight of you all, as I may say," he began, addressing the other Fir-cones. "I can see the white mountains over there with all the snow upon them, pointed peaks right up among the stars. I wonder whether they are higher than I am!"

"To be sure they are," cried a little Cone, delighted.

"Well, perhaps they are, but I can see over them, and at all events there are none of our species there, that is certain; and I can see down ever so deep. I can look down

upon you all, little dears. As for the men
and the cattle in the valleys, they are but
specks; I look right past them to the blue
lake, taking it all into my view, its width
and length, its white cliffs on one side, its
little towns and villages, its churches, its vine-
clad hills, the boats on its blue waves, and
the ranges of hills beyond. I can see it all,
and a great deal more; only I like best to
look straight down and see all that lies at
my feet. There's a running stream dashing
over the rocks right down hundreds and
hundreds of feet below me, but I can hardly
stop to notice its voice, it is so much beneath
me. I like better to listen to the music of
the wind in our countless fir-trees, and to feel
that it is all my own. Somebody says that
the fir-trees are the harp of the universe,
playing in harmony to the joys and sorrows of
the world, and I think he was right—I do!"

Would not Lamartine have been proud if he had only known of the Fir-cone's approbation! He made a little pause here, for even boasting is bad sport if nobody will answer you. So he took to the question form of speech, hoping to provoke a reply.

" Young Acorn, down there," he shouted, clearing his throat first, " I don't know whether I can make you hear, but I want to know if you would not like to change places with me?"

" Places?" answered the Acorn, catching at the only word he could hear. " Oh, yes, I know of lots of places! Do you want a place? You must be out of place up there, I am sure. What can you do, run errands?"

" Dear me, how stupid!" cried the Fir-cone; then he shouted contemptuously, "who taught you to make low jokes, eh?"

But the Acorn did not hear.

"Beech-nuts!" he shrieked by-and-by, "which of you would like to come and spend a day with me?"

The wind carried his message this time and brought back the answer.

"The little ones are not to make a noise up-stairs, the Beech-nuts are busy talking."

This was very provoking, especially as all the little Fir-cones began to titter. However, he whistled to hide his vexation, and then began to sing :—

"I can see right over to England,
  And out of England into France,
  And out of France into Spain,
  And over the hills and home again!"

"No, you can't," answered a member of the Alpine Club, who chanced to be resting under this tree, and who had just had bad news from home. "If you could, I'd change places with you. But there is no England to be seen from where you are, worse luck!"

" Hushaby baby on the tree-top," cried all the little Fir-cones. "We mustn't tell stories, however high and mighty we are."

" I can't hear you, it's no use talking all that way down," cried the boaster, feeling very hot and angry.

"Poor little fellow," murmured a sunbeam who happened to pass at that moment, " he's all alone up here in the cold, I must stay and warm him a bit."

It was not exactly what he wanted at that moment, yet the little attention was pleasant to his wounded pride; moreover, it gave him the chance of asking, though in a humbler tone :—

" Can you feel the sun down there ?"

There was no answer.

2

" Can you feel the sun down there?"

No answer.

" I say, can you feel the sun down there ?"

" You can't hear when we speak."

" Yet you might be polite."

It had just struck him how awful it would be if they took him quite at his word, and never spoke to him any more.

" Well, no, thank you, we don't feel the sun, but it is pleasant in the shade sometimes."

"Not always."

He was anxious to go on talking with that fear upon him.

" Not always, no ; but then we shall not be in the shade when your tree comes down, you know."

" It won't ever come down."

No answer.

" I say, it won't ever come down."

" Well, of course, you know, being so

high; but the woodman marked it this morning."

" Oh, he didn't !"

" Well, of course, you know, being so high, but there's the mark. Perhaps one may be a little too high to see some things. However, it makes one hoarse to scream, and besides, you know, you can't hear what we say."

And they wouldn't say another word.

All that night the little green Fir-cone thought it over, wishing with all his might that he could see this one thing. After all, what was the use of being able to look across mountains, and lakes, and forests if one couldn't see the marks of ruin on one's own supports ? But it is the way with some of us. The cold clouds wrapped round the hill that next morning, and though the little fellow knew that he was the first of all the forest Cones to catch sight of the first red peep of sunrise, he was feeling so chilled, and sad, and heart-achy, that he could not bring himself to an-nounce the fact.

By and by the friendly sunbeam passed again with the same kind words :—

"Poor little fellow, he is all alone up here in the cold. I must stop and warm him a little."

And it stopped and dried up all his tears, and all the cold, damp chill of terror that had come over him. Then he fell back into his old song.

"Why, you Sky-lark!" he said to a mounting bird, "don't you wish you were up here without the trouble of mounting, like me, for instance."

"Oh, not like you, please, not like you!" sang the bird; "fancy being all stuck up in th: clouds here, and no chance of going down to the nest."

THE FIR-CONE.

"But you might have your nest up here," persevered the Fir-cone, "It would be nice."

"Oh, thank you, no," said the Lark, "it would be most unhealthy for the young ones; besides having a tendency to give them high notions!"

"What sort of high notions? I thought it was your family nature to fly high!"

"Yes, but not to be high to begin with."

"Do you know if the woodman ever comes as high as this, Sky-lark?"

"He's just coming, your tree is marked, and he is just coming with his axe."

"But they don't cut down trees on the tops of mountains," said the little Cone, very faintly.

"Mountains! This isn't a mountain, it's only a hill called a mountain for courtesy. I'm going ever so much higher to the real mountain peaks. You're not half so high up as you think, for all your boasting!"

Terrible mistake, discovered too late! He was not so high as he thought. He was not beyond the reach of the woodman! How he did tremble when he heard the woodman's whistle.

"Acorn, oh Acorn! won't you change places!" he shrieked at the top of his voice, but the Acorn could not hear.

"Brother Cones, oh, brother Cones, help me!"

But there came a little tittering laugh, and that was all the answer he got.

Then he burst into burning tears, for there came a sharp blow of the axe, which sent a shiver up to the topmost tip of the pointed fir tree.

"I thought I was out of reach of this!" he sobbed. "I thought I was beyond such ruin!"

"Thought, thought, you sham!" said a passing gust of wind; "why did you presume to think? why didn't you find out?"

"Cling tight to me," said the Twig he was growing on, "if only you cling we shall not fall far. They won't let the tree fall into the valley, you know, but backwards on to the hill. Cling fast."

"I can't, oh, I can't," sobbed the Green Cone, "I have stretched my neck so that I am hardly holding on at all, and I have always looked down upon things."

"Yes, that was the mistake," ran a whisper through the boughs; and, at that moment came a crack, a crash, a fall, and the tall tree was lying back on the hill. But, with one tremendous shock, the little Cone was sent bounding through the air, away, away, away.

Long afterwards he awoke from long unconsciousness to find himself on the moss by the side of the splashing stream.

"Isn't it very bad down here? Aren't you frightened?" he asked of a little Fern.

"He that is low need fear no fall," was the amused answer.

"Ah, I made a mistake once," said the Fir-cone.

III

THE LITTLE BERRY-BOYS.

YELLOW Berries—beautiful yellow Berries, they were, showing their shining faces here and there, in a certain hedge more than twenty years ago. I think they must have been very proud of themselves, those orange-coloured Berries, but I don't know quite, for I was not there to read their little looks, and hear their little sayings. But I can fancy how they looked their best, and shone their brightest, and rejoiced to think that they had got their full colour earlier than the Hips and Haws. For it was early in the autumn, before the time of heavy dews and gossamer-webs, and yellow leaves, and cold evenings.

Do you know why it was such a good thing to get ripe and golden before the Hips and Haws? Why, because, of course, in the early autumn days the birds are not so hungry; they have still a few songs left in their portfolio, and are not so greedy and peckish! But in later days, when the strawberries are done long ago, and the cherries have vanished, and peaches and plums are things of the past, ah, then the poor Hips and Haws, and all the hedge-Berries have their turn; and the sharp beaks pierce and peck, and pinch, and wound without paying the smallest attention to those wee, tiny, plaintive cries, which are the only way the flowers have of expressing pain. Indeed, those sounds are so infinitely tiny, that there are few ears beside mine that ever hear them.

Some people would persuade us that we are only fancying them, which people we do not condescend to answer. But we were talking about the yellow berries, and I was going to say how happy it was for them that they came out yellow so early in the year. I was going to say so, but I stopped myself, because I remembered that if it had been but a little later, those two large brown eyes that caught sight of them would have been far away in London. Those two brown eyes, they only belonged to a child, and yet they were large, and they had a way of gazing at things that often surprised people. Well, they caught sight of the beautiful Berries, and the busy brain behind them, which had a queer way of always concocting plans, remembered a certain small sister at home, and resolved to do something at once. It was the doom of those beautiful Berries. The busy little hands were stretching up in a twinkling, and though the Briars cried, " Berries, I'll defend you ! " and scratched with all their might ; and the Nettles said, " Berries, we'll avenge you ! " and stung as only Nettles know how—yet for all that, the little yellow fellows were carried off in triumph by the two scratched hands. And I have a sort of impression that those scratched hands, though they are a great deal bigger now, would run the risk of worse things than scratches for the sake of pleasing that same younger sister.

Poor little round Berries, they went home in a very resigned state of mind, for they knew that it is never of any use to grumble ; that, in fact, when you are in the power of one stronger than yourself, there is nothing better than to be silent and still. They were not a bit like those foolish children who provoke rough brothers to teaze them more and

more by shrieking and screaming the moment
they are touched. They were rather per-
secuted, those little rolypolies, I think. First,
they were torn apart, and pulled off their
stalks, and left to roll over and over on the
table in a helpless way. And then—and oh,
that was far the worst—they were stabbed
through the very heart, and the dagger
twisted round and round, until, when it came
out at last, you could have seen all the secrets
written on their minds—if they had any—as
easily as possible. And a little curly-wurly
snake, of white elastic, came creeping in—
through one, two, three, through all of
them, and wouldn't go out again for anything. But I shouldn't say all of them, for
there were two snakes, and they divided the
Berry-balls between them; and then the
heads and tails of the snakes were tied together. And their tormentor never thought

a bit about the heart-ache of each little yellow fellow. Let us hope they soon forgot it themselves, and never thought any more of the hedge, nor of their friends, the Hips and Haws, nor of their own stalks, nor anything. When we are turned out of our old life, and old home, the best thing, if we want to be comfortable, is to forget it, isn't it? I am not quite sure, to tell the truth.

At last, they were all packed up in a box, and they went a long journey in a train, which is certainly more than we would advise most Berries to expect, at all events. I think they were in a box, but they may have been in a pocket, it does not much matter, does it?

At the end of the journey came light again, and then the presentation; and the Berries who had made up their minds, like a certain famous man you will know by and

by, "to be jolly under all circumstances,"
looked bright and shining as ever. There
was a great deal of pleasure between
those two small sisters, in the giving and
receiving, and as the little round balls hung
round the small wrists, they whispered to
each other that "it was nice to be thought
so much of, and to make people so
happy."

All that afternoon they shared the play
that went on in that nursery; and in their
way, they laughed and chattered too. When
the happy owner of the bracelets called them
her golden balls, and talked of the wonderful
jeweller who had made them for her, after a
pattern nobody else had ever seen—all pretending, you know—they were as proud as
possible. For they fancied, poor foolish
things, that the work of some famous worker
in gold and jewels must rank higher, and

be more wonderful than the simple fruit of the trees and plants.

"What have you done with your beautiful Berries, neighbour?" asked the Hawthorn of the Creeper in the hedge.

"They have been stolen from me!" said the Creeper. "They were of such beautiful colour, that they caught the eye a little robber. You are happy that yo have your crimson glories yet to come!"

"I don't know that we have much quarrel about," was the answer. "My littl red children are eaten by the birds, your Berries are stolen by human fingers. But where are they now?"

"They are away in London, they tell me, and are likely to be much thought of there, where it seems there are not many folks like you and me."

"Much thought of for a little while, and

then, perhaps, thrown away! However, we
need not grumble; we have our day, and that
is all we need ask."

Yes, the yellow Berries had had their
day, even while their friends were talking
about them.

For there came a wise elder sister to
where the children were playing, and she
saw the bracelets, and called them a very
ugly name, which settled their fate very
quickly. It is bad enough to be shunned
like poison, or hated like poison; but to be
actually called poison is worse still. And
that was what happened to the bright Berries.
You can fancy how indignant they felt—how
they could have turned and twisted on the
snake that held them, for very shame and
anger. But there was nobody there that
could hear and understand the little plaintive
words.

"Oh, we would not hurt you! We wouldn't ever do you any harm! The little birds eat us sometimes, and they never have bad pains. And least of all would we dream of hurting you! Oh, don't throw us away!"

Nobody could hear their pleading. They looked up brightly and beamingly into their little owner's face, and she looked down at them, and believed in them with all her heart. But what was the use of that? They had been called poison, and they must be thrown away. There came a great lump in the child's throat, for she did not like to part with those beautiful bright things from the country. But the thing that seemed to choke her most was what she could not have put into words. It was just the idea that there had gone a great deal of love in the gathering of those Berries, and a great deal of thought for her in the threading of them—and now all was to be wasted. But I don't think she said much about it. The bright berries were thrown out into the London garden, and left there to rot and die. And yet somehow or other they have had a much longer life than most Berries, for they are remembered even now—twenty years and more after they died, all alone there, away from their hedge. And the strange choky feeling that came into the little sister's throat when they were thrown away, all that long time ago, is inclined to come back again.

A pert, young robin was hopping about in that hedge in the snow time, trying to make some kind of a dessert from the red haws, all sodden and cold. He had had a good dinner of crumbs at the farm window, but he pretended to be anything but content.

"What do you mean by having no

Berries this year ? " he said, saucily, to the Creeper.

" They were all stolen from me, if you please, sir, and taken up to London to be a plaything to a little girl. But they tell me she could not keep them."

" Sad, *very!* " said Master Robin. " Now if you ask *me*, that's what I call a wasted existence."

But I don't think he knew anything about it, do you ?

IV

"GLAD WE ARE WHERE WE ARE."

"Daisy, dear, it's time you went to sleep, isn't it?" said a blade of Grass one evening, in a very sleepy tone.

The Daisies are such chatterboxes, that really it is quite a comfort for the Moss, and the Dandelion-plants, and the Grass on the lawn, when they say " good-night," and shut their saucy eyes.

"Time to go to sleep," laughed this particular Daisy, " we have no special time for going to sleep in our family; you would find if you walked across the lawn that no two of us shut our eyes at the same minute. We are of too much use in the world; it wouldn't do for us all to be asleep at once, except quite after dark, when you know nothing ever happens. Why, I can tell you we are concerned, one way or another, with most things, and most people too, for the matter of that."

"Are you, Daisy, dear?" said the Grass, and nodded sleepily as it spoke, and the merry little fellow, seeing that it was of no good at all, laughed and said—

"Well, I see you are bent on it, so here goes!" and he shut his eye, too, and was off as sound as a top.

Next morning, of course, he was early awake, and looking about to see how the world was going; but, as nothing particular was happening, he contented himself with wagging his head, laughing in the sun's very face, and then singing quietly to himself till it got too hot to sing. By-and-by the shadows fell across him from the great trees, and he was taking a quiet, open-eyed doze, such as flowers like, when he felt two little soft fingers at his stem, and he was just picked gently off. They were very soft, rosy, little fingers, and they did not hurt him. Indeed, I do not think he minded it much, even when a sharp pin made a slit in his stalk, and he found a little brother Daisy nestling his head up against him.

"It's funny," that was all he said; and when he found himself one of a pretty chain of Daisies hanging round Baby's neck, he cooled his merry face against the white pinafore, and looked very well pleased. Baby didn't know, for he couldn't hear, and wouldn't ever have understood the queer little talk that went on round his neck. A kind of round game, you know, that was better than "cross questions and crooked answers," or any of those things that one always gets so tired of playing.

"Well, I call this rather good fun," said one little fellow.

"It's ever so much cooler than out there in the sun," said his neighbour, whose spot in the grass had been just outside the shade.

"To think what we might have come to," said one who was rather sentimental.

"My brother lost his head by the mowing-machine yesterday," said the next, "and so should I have, if I had not bowed down till my neck nearly broke."

"My uncle died an awful death," said the one on Baby's shoulder; "a little witch got hold of him and pulled him to pieces, petal by petal, muttering the magic words, 'this year, next year, sometime, never,' over him till the last."

"How shocking!" said his neighbour.

"Well, let us be glad we are where we are," said the Daisy, who was struggling up through the strings of the pinafore. And "Glad we are where we are," was the little song that ran round and round Baby's neck. They sang it all the evening while Baby was having his tea, and afterwards while he was at play, until at last bed-time came. I don't think the Daisies had quite settled that it was bed-time. At all events, the little fellow who was caught in Baby's fingers was very wide awake, and did not quite enjoy the squeeze he got before Baby was persuaded to say "ta-ta" to his pretty chain, and submit to be undressed. Then they were all laid down on the nursery table, and talked a little to each other while the splashing in the bath was going on.

"I'm rather thirsty," said one, "I should

like to be out-of-doors, drinking up the dew now."

"I'm a little faint," said another, "and my stem is getting stiff. I suppose we have not much longer to live."

"No, we shall go to sleep soon," said the one whose neck had been twisted by the little fingers; "but we have had a good while together, and a better time than many Daisies."

"Glad we've been where we've been," was the good-night, sleepy song, and then they all sighed softly, and went to sleep there on the nursery-table. Somebody said something about putting them in water to keep them fresh till the morning, but nobody did it.

In the middle of the night, there was a great bustle in the nursery. There was hurrying backwards and forwards, whispers, and louder talking, a pouring out of hot water, and a great deal of confusion. All of a sudden a heavy tray was put down on half the Daisy-chain, and the rest of the Daisies woke with a start.

" I feel all hot and parched up," said a little Daisy in a weak whisper, " do you remember the cool dew and the pleasant grass ? "

" Do you remember the nice cool pinafore?" asked another, " perhaps they'll put us on that again ?"

" Perhaps they will. Good-night, I'm tired."

But they didn't; no, little Baby never wore the Daisy-chain again. Next morning the nursery was very still and quiet, and nobody noticed the withered flowers. They had said good-night and gone to sleep after their short happy time of it, and they wouldn't wake up any more—not any more at all.

And little Baby, little rosy, merry Baby had gone to sleep after his short, happy time, gone to sleep for a long, long while; but who could say that he would not wake any more? For Baby's life was very different to the Daisy's life, wasn't it?

Nurse found the chain when she came to move the tray, and she took it up quickly.

"Deary me, now, it's his Daisy-chain," she said, "and to think he wore it only yesterday!"

But the little Daisies did not know that she cried over them, and hid them away with sundry little treasures in a drawer. Because, you see, they were fast asleep. They stayed there, hidden away, for a long, long time.

But there were other Daisies where they

THE DAISIES.

came from, and there are other Daisies all
about in the fields and over the lawn and
under the trees. Dear me, they are as
common on the earth as the stars are in the
skies, or as little children in the houses.
When the winter came they disappeared,
and their place was covered up by the snow,
and people forgot that they had ever been.
But by-and-by the summer came back, and
they were peeping out everywhere. Wherever there was the least bit of sun, there
the Daisies grew, on the open lawn and in
the wide field, and in the churchyard
grass. Aye, in the churchyard grass !
There was a little, small green mound
there that a lady came to visit one day;
and as she stooped down over it, and
murmured sweet words about Baby, the
little Daisies on the tiny grave looked straight
up in her face, not merrily this time, per-

haps, but, oh, so happily, as if they had something sweet and bright to sing about the happy life of little flowers here, and little Baby, too, in the far away world.

"We might clear away all the Grass and Daisies, and plant roses and lilies instead ; but I don't think we will," the lady said. "The Daisies make me think of that Daisy-chain I made him, and they remind me of him, so bright, and wee, and happy they look. I am glad they are where they are."

Yes, that was just the Daisies' own song, " Glad they are where they are."

And by-and-by the lady added, but softly to herself, " And I'm glad he is where he is, my little wee flower, in the sweet fields beyond the river."

And the Daisies looked up and almost seemed to smile.

V

THE FIGHT.

IT wasn't a flower, properly speaking; they called it a weed, but it was not that in the usual sense of the word—it was a Sea-weed. And that is just the sort of thing which I think it would be most delicious to be this terribly hot weather.

I believe it had a long Latin name, if the truth were told; but you don't know Latin, no more do I, so we won't call it by its name. We will just call it young Sea-weed. Can you fancy anything half so beautiful as it was? Lying in its native pool, cosily resting among the other Sea-weeds, and floating on the cool, bright water—spread out with its red, fine branches and twigs, and fibres, all of the tiniest, fairy-like kind. And it had plenty to do and plenty to see, fastened as it was to its home-rock. For there were the tiny crabs playing at "hide and seek," underneath it, just as you do in the shrubbery, you know. And there were the shrimps making it a starting-place for their exciting races, or calling it "home," when they had a game at "hare and hounds." And there were the shell-fish, so tiny that you could hardly see them, nestling themselves in the thickest part of it. Indeed, I rather think that if that young Sea-weed could have told its own story, it would have had to describe little live things that lived, and eat, and drank, and enjoyed themselves all among its branches, yet too small for any human eye to see them.

But I can only tell you what I know; and I am very sure that I shall not be able to tell you half the wonders that might be told if we knew all the secrets of our young Seaweed. Let me tell you what I can fancy happened to it one time when nobody was looking.

It was quite in the middle of the night, and the tide was low, and the sea ever so far away, lying under the moon, which was just going to set behind its bright, sleepy waters. And it was the crabs' happiest play-time. Now, don't be surprised, but just think a minute. You say there was a low tide in the middle of the day as well as in the middle of the night, when they might come out on the sand, or scramble over the rocks without any great waves to sweep over them. Well, of course there was, and then there were plenty of little boys and girls on the rocks, too, ready to catch them with their nets, or pick them up with their fingers, or knock them with their spades. Oh, you little goose, can't you see that the crabs must keep all their best fun for the night low-tide, when they have all the room to themselves, and nobody to disturb them?

Well, the young Sea-weed was lying happily enough in the moonshine, stretching out its arms as far as possible into the cool water, and drinking in all the nice moisture at its roots. And then it didn't mind a bit if the little live creatures came and nibbled at it. Almost all things, except human things, are made to be eaten, some alive, some after they are dead, and they don't grumble, any of them. No more did the Sea-weed. It was just lying watching the shrimps at their games, and letting the tiny creatures suck at its leaves, or tumble about in its branches, just as they liked; when, all of a sudden, two large crabs came across the rock in opposite directions. They had got their pincers up in the air, and their eyes were standing half out of their heads, and they were looking very fierce indeed. Now, of course, you know, if you are not quite a goose, that the crabs are the sea-soldiers. They wear armour, strong and stiff; and they have sharp weapons which they know how to use. The worst of it is, that they are very much given to civil war, which, you know from your history, is a very bad kind of war indeed. Only in this case, perhaps, it may be just as well that the sea-soldiers should keep down their numbers by fighting amongst themselves, lest the whole sea-beach should turn into a military despotism, which, as of course you know, would never do. Well, these two crabs had a good cause of quarrel, or thought they had. I believe they had been passing under a large stone at the same time, and neither would give way to the other; and so, of course, as any school-boy will see, it was a case of honour, and must be fought out.

And the young Sea-weed laughed at the prospect. Just to lie still that hot night, and see other people exciting themselves, was such very good fun. A limpet, on the rock, lifted a side of its shell and asked what was the matter. An anemone, very busy looking out for its supper, sighed to think of the disturbance, which would frighten away all passing eatables, and shut itself up to think about it. And the shrimps took to flight. "Go it," cried the little crabs, and hid themselves, laughing, in our young Sea-weed.

Then both champions stood up on their hind legs, and looked very fierce, and very

THE FIGHT.

awful, and one said, " Now, sir !" and the other said, "Come on, sir !" and the tug of war began. And the young Sea-weed laughed—laughed in all its fibres, giggled from root to tip. Oh, the wicked young Sea-weed !

They fought, and fought, and fought ! As for black eyes and bleeding noses, such as you boys understand, they are all a trifle to it. There was a clatter of arms that awoke the sleeping starfish, and angry words, not loud, but deep, that made the very jelly-fish shudder ! By-and-by, there was the horrid crash of a breaking claw, and the little crabs hid their faces, frightened; but still the Sea-weed quivered with merriment. Oh, the wicked young Sea-weed ! There was a pause in the fight—a little breathing time, you know—and the angry combatants looked at each other in deadly hate, and then looked at the joints of their armour. I don't know which was the stronger, nor which was the braver, nor which was most likely to win. But when they called for another round, and rushed in blind fury at each other's eyes, perhaps the rock was slippery even for crabs —perhaps the moonlight dazzled their sight; perhaps— But never mind why it was; they fell struggling, and fighting, and furious, right into the midst of the young Sea-weed, and vanished under the water. And the young Sea-weed, torn and rent from its roots, tossed about hither and thither in the terrible fight — the young Sea-weed laughed no longer.

And the moon went down, and it was all dark, and by-and-by the sea crept over the stones, and covered them all. The long hours went by, one by one, and again the sand came in sight, and the green rocks.

And in a certain little pool lay a maimed and wounded crab, looking sadly enough at its two legs, far away in the water, and thinking of its conqueror gone off in triumph. And the young Sea-weed? Oh, the wicked young Sea-weed—torn up by the roots, was gone—gone away on the ocean, nobody knows where—nobody knows how!

VI

HOW TO USE ONE'S PRICKLES.

I HAVE heard of a man something like my-self. Something like myself, I say, because he loved the flowers with that uncommon kind of love that means sympathy. He put himself in the place of the flowers, and fancied to himself what the flowers must feel. Only I think he rather overdid his fancying, for he thought that they must be so hurt when their prettiest bunches were cut off, that as he went through the wood filling his hands with blue-bells and primroses, he thought he heard every plant shrieking after him, until the whole place was one chorus of lamentation. Poor little flowers, it isn't so bad for them as all that, and yet it must be rather bad sometimes when careless children pick them and throw them down in the dust to die, instead of giving them a chance in a glass of water at home.

A sad, sad sigh, I heard from a large white Convolvulus one day :

" I was looking so bright and beautiful," she said ; " I had climbed up to the very top of the hedge, and it was so nice up there. And it was only this morning that I spread out my great white face to take it all in. Oh, dear, why did that dreadful boy come and tear me all down, and leave me here among the Nettles ? Shall I ever get up again ? "

" No; there isn't a chance for you," sang the Nettles ; but they sang it cheerily. " You will have to lie here in our laps and rest. And we'll take the choicest care of you, lady fair! Don't you know us, Flora's brave lancers? Only let the little robber touch you now, and he shall have more than he likes!"

The white beauty thanked them but faintly, for she was wounded and weak. The talkative Nettles went on among themselves.

"Queer enough there was nobody up there to protect her ladyship—not one among all those high-born flowers to give blow for blow, or do a mischief when needs be! That's all that comes of being aristocratic, you see; injured innocence has to look to us common folks for protection."

"Well now, I do declare now," began a simpering voice over their heads, and looking up the Nettles saw the affected young guardsman, Nightshade, flaunting his gay regimentals over them, and drawling away in his own fashionable tone.   They laughed, but he went on—

"Look here, now, what could you fellows do for a lady, now?   If you were put to it, now?   A few stings?   Aye, who'd care for that?   Look at me, now, you know what I'm good for?"

"Oh, to be sure, to be sure," sneered the Nettles, "if anybody would take the trouble to eat you, you'd kill them!   And very clever of you, to be sure!   But suppose they should not take the trouble?"

"Well, there now, I'm not so touchy as you fellows, I confess!   It isn't handling me that hurts, it's injuring me.   But, come now, it is no good soldiering to carry your sword with its point out, come now!"

"Oh, enough, enough!" cried a Holly-bough, whose face was all shining with good humour. "No quarrelling, I pray. We've all got our place in the Queen's court, and we all know our duty without talking about it."

"I wonder what my duty is?" said a merry bunch of May.

"Why, to look pretty and smell sweet, my darling," said the Holly-bough.

"I believe I'm one of the poisonous chaps," called out the Dandelion, in his hoarse, unrefined tone of voice.

"If you are, it's very likely you can give medicine too, for aught I know," said the Holly-bough; and he spoke the truth without knowing it, perhaps.

"Well, this lady fair has missed her vocation, at all events," said the Nettles, as they tossed the Convolvulus in the wind. "Look, she'll be dead in no time!"

"Don't you be rough with her," answered the Holly-bough; "perhaps she has a chance yet. And mind, if anybody comes to save her, don't send them off with your clumsy stings !"

The Nettles laughed, for they were proud of their spears; but they answered with the old joke—"We don't sting this month, you know." But they took the hint for all that.

It was not five minutes after that that a little girl came past with her big brother. The little girl noticed the beautiful flower, and cried out—

"Oh, I wish I could get that splendid Convolvulus for my hat; but it's all among the nasty Nettles."

How hot and uncomfortable the Nettles felt !

"I will get it for you," said the big brother. And he stretched out his walking-stick, and lifted the drooping beauty gently out of her friends' arms. Then he twined it round and round the broad-brimmed hat.

"You must make haste home," he said, " and give the poor thing some water."

And all the flowers looked after her, envying her.

" She won't live long," said the Nettles, as if they liked to think so.

"But she will see the world, at all events, and give pleasure into the bargain," said the Dandelion. " Nobody ever dreams of taking us home with them." He was rather envious.

" People don't take me either, now," yawned the Nightshade; "it would be at their peril now."

"People do take me," cried the Holly-bough, "at least, they will when Christmas comes. And won't I have fun then, and see merry faces, and watch grand games, and hear happy carols, and help to make them all the happier. And you'll come, too, old fellow," he shouted to a Mistletoe in an apple-tree, not far off. "Ha, ha, we'll have a fine time of it." And he went on with all his pleasant thoughts of the future, talking in his own good-humoured fashion; and all the flowers listened.

"Yet you have got prickly points, and you can hurt people, too!" said the Nettles, as if they were a little jealous.

"Yes, so I have, and so has the Rose its thorns, but that doesn't matter. People know how to handle us, and we don't hurt it we can help it."

"No; we don't hurt if we can help it," sang all the little Roses, all down their thorny bough.

And the Nettles thought it was a good hint, and made up their minds that they, too, wouldn't hurt if they could help it.

VII

WHAT'S THE USE?

"WHAT *is* the use of it all?" that was the burden of the long, soft sigh that went up on the hot, mid-day air from the heathery hill. For the little Heath-cups were very hot—the sun poured down all his scorching rays upon them; and the Fir-trees, though they looked so cool and pretty, were a long way off, and could not stretch their shadows half far enough to shield them in the very most trying time. It is true there was a soft breath of sea air coming over the cliffs; but the sea, too, was a long way off, and only gave them a salt mouthful of air every now and then.

And the ground was getting very hard and dry, cracking all over with the heat; and the grass seemed all dead and gone, it was so brown. So the little Heath-bells, nodding to each other in their feverish state, whispered that at any rate it was healthy weather, just suited to their peculiar constitutions—trying to make the best of it, you know, for they were very hot, and felt as if they were growing redder in the face every minute. And it was all very true; nothing could be more wholesome and robust than the strong, sweet breath of health, which the sun drew out of those little fellows. Only what is good for us is not always pleasant. The Peach might well exult in his beautiful rosy cheek, and yet not quite enjoy the long hours inside his hot blanket, roasting on a hot wall. So the sigh came over and over again from the little Heath-bells, "What *is* the use?"

And I began to wonder myself what the use could be, as I listened to the feverish, restless movement all around me. I thought of the comfortable life of the heath-plants in the greenhouse, shaded, and watered, and aired, and heated, just as every hour's need arose. And these poor little wild things seemed to have a hard time of it, all to no purpose. For what can be the use of a flower except to live happily and look pretty all the few days of its life?

To suffer with a purpose may be all very well; to be roasted alive to no purpose is quite a different thing! But is there any suffering to no purpose in this world? Is there any?

So I lay on my back, with shaded face, listening to the distant lark far overhead; and I wondered if the Heath-bells could catch the cool music in his song, that always seems like the ripple of flowing water—so refreshing and nice. Then he turned and came down. I thought he would surely have his nest in the long, waving hay, hard by; and I thought of the coming scythe, and pitied him. But he made a sudden turn to one side, and hovered long and lovingly over the thickest bed of purple heather. And the fag-end of the song he was singing, the song that took in every joy of his happy life, his morning hymn, and his hunting-song, and his verse to the sun, and his " Home, sweet home,"—the fag end of that song was not in praise of the golden gorse, but in love of the beautiful heather which circled his little ones' cradle. " So warm, so bright, so sweet-breathed," he called it; and the Heath-bells looked up at him, and never sighed out, " What's the use ? "

But he settled down in his nest and was

silent; and the terrible sun seemed fiercer and fiercer, as the noon passed into the afternoon. There was a great silence all over the heath—such a great silence that you could not hear ever a murmur in the Fir-trees, nor a sigh from the Heath-bells. The gay butterflies and the dragon-flies seemed to be the only creatures that had energy to move; and nothing, you know, will ever keep them at home, such gad-abouts they are! "Hot, so hot, and not a breath to breathe," murmured the Heath-bells, and then they fell into a drowsy state, and said no more.

By-and-by, there was a little stir—a click of the latch of a distant cottage-door, a sound of footsteps coming and then going away. I did not know what it meant, and I did not care.

But after a little while I found that there

THE HEATH-BELLS.

were new-comers all around me—here and there, in ones and twos. Little happy, humming bees, they were—very happy, of course, and full of eager chat. "We are all coming, pretty Heath-bells," I heard them say; "they have brought out our hive, and we shall have such fun! There is no honey like yours, pretty Heath-bells; we are all come to gather it fast. You have the sweets of all the flowers, and mountain air, and sea-breezes as well, you rich little fellows! And you are keeping it safe for us, too, and will let us come and feast to the full! How long have you waited to feed us, standing up in the sun on the breezy hill-side, growing rich every hour to feed us? How long have you waited, little Heath-bells?"

But they never stopped for an answer, they went in and out, over and under, round and round; and the bees and the bells understood each other, and fed and feasted happily and long. I must not tell you all their secrets, all the confessions of the little purple boys—all the merry murmurs of the little brown-coats. Hours passed away while they were cosing together, giving and taking, whispering loving words, and nodding funny nods to each other.

And, meantime, the hot sun was going down behind the cliff—dipping his glowing face into the blue, blue sea, and throwing back great floods of glory all over the sky. But those floods of glory had nearly faded out, before the brown bees said " Goodnight " to the purple bells, and went home satisfied. And when I looked in the clear, cool twilight, there was a dew-drop bright, in each little heath-cup, as if they were sorry they had ever whispered murmuring words in the mid-day heat.

And I wondered whether any others, besides the heather-bells, ever said, " what's the use ?" in the burning noontide, and found it all out at the evening-time!

VIII

FORTUNE-TELLING.

THE Thistle-down is the flowers' gipsy-woman, and tells them their fortunes. Did you know that? I dare say not, for I sometimes think you wouldn't know any-thing about the flowers if it was not for me. Of course, you might know botany, but that isn't knowing about the flowers, any more than studying skeletons is making friends. Think now, all their little ways and their fancies and their fidgets, what would you know about them if it was not for me? And yet people say—they do!—that I don't care for the sweet things, because I never gather great bunches and go about with my hands full. Well, there are some folks who cannot understand that you love your friends unless they see you always hand in hand with them or gazing at their photographs; they don't understand hidden sympathies, and, poor things, they probably never will! They have not the higher nature, you see.

But I was going to tell you about old Dame Thistle-down and her fortune-telling. She was a great favourite with the younger and gayer flowers, who looked upon her rare visits as great fun, though their more sober elders and betters contended that she was a worthless vagrant, and ought never to be admitted to a respectable garden. Which was, I dare say, true; yet, for all that, those flowers whose happy homes bordered on the wild common, which was her proper home, thought themselves very fortunate, and were always on the watch for the wind which was likely to bring her their way. I was very much amused one day at her visit to a rocky garden rather over-crowded with flowers, most of whom were eager to get a word with her.

" And what is to happen to me, mother?" asked a fresh young Moss-rose.

" Ye are to have a happy home in a wine-glass, and to be much minded for memory's sake."

" And little me, granny?" asked a bit of Mignonette.

" Ye, my darlint, ah, there's a sweet love waiting for ye, and a plenty of kisses."

"" We know all the fine things in store for us, without any gipsy cunning," said the gaudy China Asters.

" It's a shower of rain and a ruin that's

waiting for ye, a pitiful death and a shameful burying," said the old thing angrily.

"Have you nothing better for me?" asked a handsome Fuchsia, somewhat anxiously, though he disdained to let it be seen.

"A prize at the flower-show, me bonny boy, but only a second prize."

"And what for this beautiful crimson Geranium, granny? It's the splendidest of us all."

The old dame paused, hovering in mid air, and watching to see if the Geranium would condescend to ask for himself, but he looked indifferent. At last she said, with an air that was infinitely mysterious—

"Early destruction, and a long surviving; ill-treatment, and a tender cherishing; a dark time, and a long one in the midst of a wise world and a great one; and a year and a day to unravel it! And I wish ye all a good-morrow."

Then, with that hobbling gait that her age and the east wind always gave her, she departed.

" Well, she has given you a chapter of contradictions for your share," said the Fuchsia to the Geranium, " what do you think it means ?"

" Who knows and who cares ?" answered the Geranium, with a grand air which effectually silenced all the lesser flowers, who had just begun to find interpretations of the mystery. They thought the grand Geranium meant what he said, and wondered at his superiority to all small curiosity, little knowing, sweet innocents, how he was, in reality, puzzling his brains for an explanation of the gipsy's speech.

Of course, you and I know better than to believe such idle predictions, and we should never expect them to come true, but then what is the use of being greater than the flowers if we are not wiser? So do not despise our pretty friends if they were too ready to believe the idle gossip of a light, wandering Thistle-down. And if what she said did seem to come true, it was only by accident, or, perhaps, even she never said it. Who knows?

It was a beautiful Geranium, you could never deny that, and many people wondered to see it in that cottage garden. For the Geranium never cared to tell people that he remembered days of grandeur, when he had been among his equals in a large glass-house. It had been one of the puzzles of his puzzling life why he had been brought by his young master and planted there among the common flowers. But this at least was a puzzle which he was to have explained to him to-day.

About an hour after Dame Thistle-down had gone, there came this same young master in at the little gate, and he uttered a merry shout as he saw his flower.

"It's quite out, nurse, in its full glory! Now, then, I am going to bring it in to you my own self, as I said."

And the next moment the Geranium felt himself beheaded, and his head knew that it was to see the inside of that cottage he had been staring at ever since he was a bud.

The old nurse put on her spectacles to look at the beauty, and the little boy chattered away.

"I told you I should come and pick it for you my own self when it was ready, and now it has come out the very right day; I could not have picked it before it was quite out, and to-morrow I shall be ever so far away."

"Ah! Master Percy, and what will your old nurse do without you?"

"Let's talk it all over again," said the little man, settling himself comfortably astride her lap, with the beautiful Geranium in his fingers. It was a pity he didn't put it down, for the talk grew so interesting that he never thought what he was doing, and he pulled it about all the time, and whenever he came to anything that was "a bother" or not just as he wished, one of the beautiful petals got an awkward twitch, which was not at all good for its health. At last one came off in his hand, which made a great pause in the talk.

"Such a beauty of a flower, and I've spoilt it!" said the boy. "Well, mamma always says my things ought to be made of iron. But what is one to do when it's *in* one to break things?"

Upon which followed a loving little lecture, such as dear old nurses can give and be listened to, unlike other people. But as the boy could not look her in the face, and must have something to do with his fingers, the end of the lecture saw all the bright petals strewed in her lap.

"It wasn't any use keeping it, you know, when it had lost a leaf," he said, when he saw the mischief he had done, "but it is a pity!"

Then a bright idea came across him.

"I say, I shall put them into one of your books, and leave them there to press till I come back, and you shall show me them there! Won't that be fun? But I must find a book you don't read much, because else they would get turned out very likely."

He was not long doing that, for on the little table that stood by the wall under the picture of Percy as a baby, lay a little pile of old books, one of which was a Latin book called Virgil, kept in remembrance of Percy's papa in his schooldays. So in the very middle of that old book, which had been so long shut up there, were placed the blooming live petals of the beautiful Geranium. Which of the inferior flowers would have envied his remarkable fortune? For a little while he lay and listened to the chatter of the little master, which came faintly to him, all smothered up as he was; and then he heard a sound of many kisses—and the cottage was all quiet and still.

· And I fancy that, perhaps, it would be right to say that here ends the story of the beautiful Geranium. But the life of a flower is a strange thing, and it would be hard to say when it is dead. You certainly could not pull me to pieces like that and leave any life in me, and yet those petals certainly were alive long after they were divided. But at last, when the sap all dried up in between those dry leaves, they went to sleep, one by one—to the beautiful flower-sleep, which was never so pretty as in that ill-treated Geranium. Day after day went by, all the bright colours were gone from the flower-beds, and only black mould was there; and that was covered, by-and-by, by the snow. But every now and then, the old nurse would go and open that old Latin book, and find the place where the crimson petals lay, each in its full, bright colour, soft and downy still. So the Geranium was tenderly cherished; though, perhaps, not for its own sake altogether.

The spring came at last with its snow-

drops and crocuses, and then the hot summer. And the Geranium plant under the
window once more—it had been in the
house all the winter — had its bunch of
green buds, which at last turned into fine
flowers.

"But not as fine as he picked," said old
nurse, and she put on her spectacles to
look in the old book; but her eyes grew
dim, for her boy was ill in a foreign land.
When she looked next time, it was with old
hands trembling with joy, for he was coming
back to-morrow.

"It's a year to-day since he left me," she
said.

Next day Dame Thistle-down was telling
fortunes in the garden, and all the flowers
were eager. Did she notice the two heads
at the window, the old head and the young
one, looking into an old Latin book?

"Early destruction, and a long surviving; ill-treatment, and a tender cherishing; a dark time and a long one in a wise world and a great one; and a year and a day to unravel it! And I wish you all a good-morrow."

IX

IT IS NOT WORTH WHILE.

THEY were next door neighbours, the Buttercups and the Quaking-grass; and, like many next door neighbours, they were not the best of friends. I believe, if the truth were known, there was a little jealousy between them, and, perhaps, a little mortified vanity into the bargain. For the Buttercups had such beautiful golden faces, and the Quaking-grass wore such a modest brown coat. And then, on the other hand, the Buttercups were such little short fellows, and the

Quaking-grass was waving away far over their heads.

It was a pity. The summer air breathed so softly and sweetly across the hay-field, and the standing hay smelt, oh, so nice; it was more than a pity that all the pleasantness of the thing should have been spoilt by those jarring words.

But, after all, it was the ugly gnats that did half the mischief. They are troublesome creatures, those gnats; they are apt to make a swelling or a festering wound wherever they alight. And they always come when you are hot and tired, and easily irritated. That's how it was in the hay-field. Just when the sun had been scorching away for hours, and the air was hot and stifling, they would hover over the Buttercups and buzz away scornfully.

"Well, I never! I wouldn't be a Butter-

THE MISCHIEVOUS GNATS.

cup, to have that ugly, tall grass growing all over my head and shutting out all the air, I wouldn't!"

And then when the Buttercups tried to look bright about it, and as if they didn't mind, they would go on to remind them of the happy days before the field was shut up for hay, when they out-topped all the grass and had the fun all to themselves. And when they saw that they had done their work thoroughly, and made the little yellow boys thoroughly uncomfortable, they would dance away, all legs and wings, to whisper to the Quaking-grass.

"Well, I never did! Fancy wearing such shabby colours, and shaking and quaking all one's days! I'd rather be a Buttercup, I do declare, right down below, if I could have my way, and get a little colour in my cheeks and not look so terribly seedy. But there, there's no accounting for tastes!"

And away they would go to bite some human hand, content that they had left behind them wounds of another kind. Those nasty, mischief-making gnats!

And the irritated Buttercups stretched and stretched their necks, and cried out in vexation, "Let me look, oh, let me look out!" But the Quaking-grass stood quaking and shaking in every breeze, and bent their heads in sulky gloom.

The Clover and the Cuckoo-flowers tried to make peace, and the different grasses looked amused. At last the sun went down, and the gentle, peace-loving moon looked down on the troubled hay-field. Now, the moon brings out all that is good in the flowers. There is no such sweet time among the fields and woods, no such nice time to look out of your window and sniff in all the breath of the dear little creatures, as just at the beginning of the dark night. Yet for a long time this ugly quarrel went on. One said one thing, and another said another; the Buttercups thought it was quite time there was a change, and the Quaking-grass nodded satirically; and the Clover said, "Never mind, never mind;" and the Cuckoo-flowers tried to turn the conversation ; but the Grasses laughed and spoilt it all. And still the Buttercups grumbled, and still the Quaking-grass stood sullen. The Grasshopper began to sing, but stopped, seeing there was something wrong, and the branches of the Willow Tree stooped down to listen. The happy little Stars looked down and sang, "Hushaby, little Buttercups, time to go to sleep!" and the Evening Breeze murmured, as it ran past, "Hush, hush, it isn't good to quarrel."

But, by-and-by, when it was quite late and ever so dark, a much rougher wind came by shrieking out, " If you don't hold your tongues there, I'll shake you."

And they knew he would be as good as his word, so they were frightened and said no more. They began to think instead. And that is the best thing, after all, when we are apt to quarrel about little nothings. Towards morning, just about the darkest time, it became very cold; and you can't think what a difference that made to the feelings in the hay-field.

" Keep close," they kept saying to each other, " let's keep each other warm."

Then one Buttercup-bud timidly whispered, " I'm very glad the Grass keeps off the wind."

And his little brother answered more boldly, " It was very stupid to quarrel with such useful folks! Besides, we shall not be long together; there's the scythe coming."

"Yes, it's only for a little while, there's the scythe coming," was the murmur all over the field.

The sun began to peep over the edge of the horizon, and the sleepy Buttercups began to open their eyes and looked pleasantly up at their tall friends, and the Quaking-grass nodded pleasantly down at the yellow boys. And they all began to say, "It's only for a little while, it isn't worth while to quarrel, and there's the scythe coming."

One grave old Buttercup, much taller than the rest, was determined to grumble still, so he said with a sigh, "I wish it would come at once; it is a weary field, all full of fighting and quarrelling. There's not any peace to be had. I long to feel the scythe."

But a little, merry fellow near him took a very different view of things.

"It won't be long, but we will have plenty of good life still, ever so much sunshine, nice morning dew, and we'll be good friends, and lie down comfortably together when the scythe comes.   It won't matter who is tallest then, why should it matter now?"

So the sun looked down on a very happy hay-field that morning when he went up over the trees, and they all nodded and played together all the morning as good friends as possible.   The bees went singing and humming over them—pleasant stories of peace and honey, and sweet words those bees had to sing.

And before evening the cool, bright scythe did come, and the Quaking-grass and the Buttercups were all laid peacefully down, side by side.   They could not quarrel then who should be tallest, and they did not want to quarrel. They sank down kissing each other, and ˌthere they lay without a look or word of anger left. And I was glad some-body had ventured to say—

"It isn't worth while to quarrel, it won't be long, and the scythe is coming!"

X.

COMING OUT.

"Well, it's all over with me now, I suppose, but it seems rather hard!"

"Who are you, and what is the matter with you?" asked a Fuchsia, in answer to the plaintive little voice that came from behind him.

"I was meant to be a beautiful Garden-Poppy of the prettiest rosy-white, but it seems to me that I shall not be anything now."

"Why not?"

"Because certain meddlesome little fingers have torn open my green covering, and spread out my petals before they were ready. And now I have no strength for anything, and there is nothing for me but to die. Ah, me! I was dreaming such a sweet dream of the pleasant life that was before me, all in the dark as I was; and I was only waiting to get strong. But it's all over with me now!"

"Well, we are in something the same case," said the Fuchsia, "though, perhaps, I am stronger and can bear it better. But those meddlesome fingers have been at me, too. I was hanging straight down, as fine a young bud as you could wish to see, when all of a sudden a pair of small fingers gave me a pinch that sent me flying open when I was not half ready, and the gardener says I shall never be the beauty that I promised to be."

Then a little yellow flower spoke, one of those bright, full-coloured, round-shaped yellow flowers that lie in beds low down on the ground; I wish I could remember his name, but I can't, and there is nobody within reach that can tell me English flowers' names. It would not be of much use to you in French or Russian, would it now? Anyhow, it was a yellow flower that spoke, and he said—

"I always wear a pale, thin nightcap till the very last minute before I am ready to open my eye. It is a custom in our family, and is said to have much to do with the freshness of our complexions. Would you believe it, my nightcap was taken off my very head by those same little meddlesome fingers, and all chance for my beauty is gone."

The three flowers sighed, and were silent. By-and-by there came past a giddy Butterfly.

"Stop, stop," cried the Fuchsia, "Butterfly, I want to know, did you come out too soon?"

"I should think not," answered she,

indignantly, "I was a caterpillar for ever so long, and after that I was all bundled up in a bundle until my wings were ready: I could not come out too soon. How could I?"

And she flew away.

After a little while a young bird came to pick up a worm close down by the yellow flower.

"Little Bird, did you come out too soon?" whispered the yellow flower.

"Certainly not," said the Bird, "or I should scarcely be as strong as I am. I wanted too; though, I was always teazing to leave the nest, but mother always said:—

> 'Birdie, wait a little longer
> Till the little wings are stronger.'

and that sang me to sleep again. She told once of some meddlesome fingers that came and took one of my brothers out of the nest,

7

and how he was lame in his wings ever after. I'm glad I didn't come out too soon, now I come to think of it."

And the three flowers sighed.

"I fancy I did come out too soon," shrieked the worm, as he wriggled in Birdie's beak. But the bird flew away with him, and the flowers sighed, all three of them. They were languishing now in the heat of the sun, and feeling sadly enough what it was to have begun life without strength enough to meet its demands.

By-and-by a young girl came by and picked off the Fuchsia with two or three of its brothers, stronger and better-looking than himself. Then the day went on, and the Poppy, after two or three attempts to open out into a respectable flower, gave up and drooped and withered. When the evening dew began to fall it revived a little, yet it

The Nestlings.

could hardly lift its head to listen, when it heard its name called in the familiar voice of the Fuchsia.

"Poppy, I say, Poppy, look where I am! Isn't it a comical place to be?"

He was perched in the head-dress of the young girl who had picked him earlier in the day. The Poppy smiled a faint smile. A few minutes after it was surprised to hear its friend's name from the lips of another passer-by. It was a warm evening, you see, and people had come out from the drawing-room to take the air.

"Yes, a great piece of Fuchsia in her hair," said the voice. "Did you ever see such a thing? But she never knows how to dress herself, she came out too soon."

"How funny," thought the Poppy, "then it is not only flowers that have to do that," and it listened for more.

" Yes, and so did this little man," said another voice, " he came out too soon, or he wouldn't be in our company to-night."

" Oh, boys don't come out," said a child's voice.

" Don't they, though ! Now, I'll tell you what you are like. You're just like that Poppy there, you're all weak and pasty-faced, and you don't know how to behave yourself, nor how to hold yourself. That's a failure of a Poppy, and you are a failure of a boy."

" That Poppy ? Oh, I pulled it open this morning, that's why it looks so queer. It wasn't ready to come out ; but I always help the flowers. I pop the Fuchsias, and I un-nightcap the yellow flowers. Only the gardener doesn't like it if he finds it out."

" I should think not. It spoils the flowers as they are spoiling you, letting you be up at this time of night, and going into company when you ought to be hidden away in the schoolroom. You'll be a failure of a boy, I tell you, just as that is a failure of a Poppy. It is just what it always comes to, cutting short the ' getting-ready time.' "

Then they passed on, but the Poppy hung its head, thinking of its happy " getting-ready time," and feeling very sure that it had never wanted it cut short. The Poppy took it more to heart than the yellow flower did, I think. He had gone to sleep and forgotten it, and there was a chance for him that he would wake up strong to-morrow, and be not much the worse for it. But then he had been nearly ready to throw off his nightcap, and the Poppy was not anything like ready to come out. Oh, I don't know anything more melancholy that that pulling open all its petals, when they ought to have been all rumpled up inside the strong green cover.

Did you ever see the wrinkles in the face of a pointer-puppy? How do you think it would like it if you tried to pull them all out and give him a long face like his mother's? Well, that was just what they had done to the Poppy. Yet it was some satisfaction to think, as it drooped, and faded, and died a failure of a flower, that it was possible that the same thing might happen to the meddlesome little boy. If they cut short his " getting-ready time " and made him come out too soon, he might turn out just as ugly, and distorted, and un-natural a thing, he might be " a failure of a boy."

Revenge is sweet, you know, even if it ought not to be.

XI

TWINED AND UNTWINED.

THERE was a steep piece of sea-cliff once which was overgrown with short Bushes, and Brambles, and such-like creatures some little way down from the top. There was a good deal of May there in the summer, and a great many Blackberries, with a funny salt taste in them, in the autumn; and plenty of Sloes, too, for those who like them. It was a kind of wild tangle, in fact, of all such vegetation as does not object to a rough sea-breeze sometimes.

A tremendous sou'wester was blowing one day; it brushed up all the leaves and made

the short, stumpy Bushes look like so many
cats' backs rubbed the wrong way. But it's
an ill wind that blows nobody any good.
That tempest did a thing which nobody ever
guessed and you mustn't tell. It caught the
loose end of a Briony wreath and flung it
right over a Convolvulus. And a little while
afterwards these two were clinging round and
round each other, as if they had been friends
all their lives, and so they vowed they would
be. Foolish things, they didn't know that

> " There's much that comes to us in life,
>   But more is taken quite away ;"

they thought they might promise for themselves and each other, that they would never
forget, never grow cold, never get separated,
never, never cease to love, and all that kind
of thing.

Well, it was very nice, and the sap in

each young thing ran merrily up and down, and in and out from the earth to the last point of the last leaf, and life was very sweet indeed. At night they slept in each other's arms, and all day long they played together. Oh, yes, that is easily said, but when one comes to describe the minutiæ of the thing, as they call it, then words fail me! How the Convolvulus talked of her white flowers to come, and the Briony told of her berries bright; how they laughed together, giggling at the teazing summer breeze that playfully puffed away, pretending that it was going to separate them; what little loving looks they interchanged when it was getting too dark for anybody to see; what indignant scorn they poured out upon the Nightshade who laughed at their friendship, calling it sentimental; what grave, earnest thoughts they had about the grand far-off sea, and how they told them to

each other; how they studied each other's
wishes as to turning certain leaves to the sun
or shade; how they went to sleep and dreamed
about each other, and then woke up and
kissed each other—oh, indeed, I can't tell it
you all, you must guess it for yourselves; and
sooner or later you will understand by expe-
rience what I mean.

" My little dears," the Nightshade said,
"it will never answer! You were both of you
made to cling to something stronger, and you
can't hold each other up. It will never do!"

" Let them alone," said the yellow Gorse,
who admired the prettiness of the thing,
" they won't do each other any harm."

The white sea birds passing that way
noticed them and laughed their own funny
laugh, half pleased, half scornful, for it was
strange to see this intertwining. The Bees
hummed round and round them — hardly

dared to tell them secrets, as they did the other flowers, lest they should tell each other. And the giddy Butterflies confessed that there was something here too deep for them to understand—their brains, you know, are not their strongest part. As for the Lark, he went and told the pale morning moon all about it, and promised to bring back a new love-song, but he never did. He forgot.

Well, the time went on, and it was a very happy time. I suppose I had better not tell you all the sweet things they said to each other, because sweets are likely to make one sick if they are not meant for oneself. They were quite sure that they were originally intended for each other, and wondered how they had ever lived through so much time apart. But for the future there could be no doubt.

"I shall never want to let you go," the

Convolvulus said, doubtfully, "I feel so sure that I was just made to lean on you, and I should be so wretched all alone."

"I can trust for the future, my sweet," said the Briony; "those whom I wish to keep I never lose; I shall not change, let all the winds blow ever so hard."

And then they would talk of something else. But the Convolvulus, poor, clinging thing! could never feel quite sure. It seems strange now to think of those days long ago, now that it all has happened. Of course, they had other things to do besides this sweet talk; there were new leaves to put forth, fresh tendrils to throw out, and the sunshine and sea air to take in and give out, and all that business with the oxygen and carbonic acid gas that wise people talk about, had to be managed. But there are a many things in this world all the better done for a little under-current of love kept flowing all the while.

It was as bright a day as you can fancy when it all happened. I think it was the end of July or the beginning of August. They had been very close together, and some people might have thought that they were more to each other than ever. And now, I am puzzled to tell you what happened, because I can't make it out myself, and never shall. It might have been an insect-hunter's net that came in between them, or it might have been a hedge-sparrow, or it might have been a gust of wind, or it might have been a passing climber's careless hand. I don't know; but when the sun went down that night, they were lying apart on the bit of bushy hedge, and apart they have been ever since. The Convolvulus held very tight, and was sorely handled in the wrench, for there are scars about her, and seamed wounds in her stem where the sap ran at the time, and, I think, she will always have these marks. But it would seem that the Briony found it easier work, and has not suffered much, from all that I can hear. They are not far apart even now, and the Convolvulus has spread out her leaves once or twice to the wind, hoping that it would carry her back to within reach. For she is cold all alone, and wants something to cuddle. And many a wistful glance she throws towards the Briony, but gets no answering look. Perhaps the Briony is busy with her bright berries, that are hanging now in beautiful bunches. Perhaps she is clinging to something else, I think that is likely. But the Convolvulus looks out to the blue, blue sea and wonders, and thinks now of the things that "life has taken quite away," puzzled.

She has other things to do still.   It is her nature to cling, you know, and her tendrils are twining fast round a stronger holding than that she has lost.   She has had some beautiful white flowers, and a great many bright, sunshiny, happy days since that day in July or August.   She does not fret, and fade, and pine away, only she looks out to sea and wonders.   Because, you know, there are so many things to remember that seem to have lost their meaning.

Perhaps some great big storm will come and drag them both together again, and set them to the dear old work of twisting round and round and twisting on to each other again.   But then very likely it won't.

"I told you it would never answer," said the Nightshade.   "I always knew how it would be."

"Then you belong to a very disagreeable

set of people," said the good-natured Gorse, " I hate the people that always know mischief is coming. For, myself, I don't know yet how it will be, but I mean to hope."

And the sea-birds noticed, but didn't laugh; and the Butterflies never stopped to wonder; the Bees told their secrets to each, but I hope they were out of their reckoning; and the Lark went away for the love song, and has not come back yet. And I don't know how it will end; do you think I may venture to hope?

XII.

THE HARVEST FIELD.

HE was thinking it all over. That was what made him bend his head, that ear of ripe wheat in the sheaf! Talk of his bending because he was over ripe! It was not that, it was just the weighty grains of thought that made the yellow husk stoop down so low, and almost broke the straw that was brittle enough to the touch. He was thinking it all over, of course he was.

And you need not laugh. His had not been the brief uneventful life of the passing flower, born to be pretty, to bloom, and to fade. He had come above ground for a pur-

8

pose, and it had taken, as the moralists say, a mingling of rain and sunshine, of cold and damp and heat, to fit him for that great purpose as he now was fit.

And that waiting in the field was just the time he wanted to think it all over. It would all be hurry and excitement by-and-by. There would be the carting away, and if his had the happiness to be the topmost sheaf, there would be all the fun of harvest cheers, and harvest songs, and the noisy, sunburnt labourers all round. And after that there was a process indistinct enough to his mind at present, but not pleasant for all its indistinctness—the threshing-machine, or the heavy flail to wrench and work him hither and thither. No, the future will not always bear looking at too closely; but the past?—oh, that is different!

The first thing he could remember was a

curious peep across the brown field, when he was quite a little fellow, and found it hard to look over a small stone that got in the way of the view. Those were very early days, and he was a wee, tender-hearted thing then, sensitive to the touch, and ready to start and tremble if a friendly slug did but crawl by him. How long ago it seemed, looking back from the harvest field! He laughed now to think of that day when a bird, pecking at a grain near him, had startled him nearly out of his wits. "Not me, Mr. Bird; oh, please, not me!" he had said, afraid of being eaten up. He who knew the meaning of a sickle now, and who had the flail in prospect!

But he had been kindly treated, and he thought of it gratefully. Just when he was at the most delicate, critical age, when the shrill winds might have blighted him, or the heavy thunder-drops have crushed him, there came the soft, soft snow, covering him down so snugly, and hushing all his childish sorrows in its warm cloak. That part of his life seemed a dream, or rather a dreamless sleep, as he looked back upon it.

· After it came the growing time—the time when every day made a difference in his height and strength. What a happy time he had of it then! He was too big to be afraid of birds or slugs, too young to think of any trouble in store. He just took the long, happy spring days one after the other, without counting them, and enjoyed them. What if the scarlet Poppy, growing near him, taunted him with his own very existence! "If your land was good, I should not be here! Nobody can look over the field and see all our red faces, and not know what a poor crop you will be. And there will be plenty more of us as the season goes on!"

Well, let the Poppies laugh, what did it matter?

"You are getting so tall," said the wee, little Pimpernel; "you will never hear me when I speak, and I can't speak loud, I'm such a little one!"

"Oh, I shall always hear you, my pet," he had answered. "I must go on growing, you know; but I'm not one of those that forget the friends of their youth." That was what he had said. How strange it seemed to remember it in the harvest field!

That was the time, too, of the birds' songs, when, as he waved in the morning breeze, he heard the Blackbird's music, ever the same, as he hunted for his breakfast. And at night, as he stood tall and cool in the moonlight, he listened to the Nightingale singing all the little birds to sleep in the copse close by. That was the time, when the Lark built his nest at his very feet, and fed his babies down there, in the sweet smell of the juicy young wheat. Ah, he remembered that sad day when the Lark had gone up to sing to the clouds, as he always did, and had never come back again, but had been made into lark-pie for somebody's dinner !

How much he had wished to comfort the widow and orphans in the nest, but had not been able to stoop low enough, which is sometimes the case with others besides the tall Ear of Corn. At last the little Larks had grown strong enough to leave the nest, and had flown off to look for their lost father.

The reapers came across the nest the very moment the sickle cut down our friend. But then it had been empty ever so long. Standing in the sheaf there, he remembered it all.

It was not quite so pleasant to look back to the days of middle age. Those days when he was beginning to get a little tired of life—when the sap did not run quite so fast up and down—when the grain was getting perceptibly harder, and he was grown to his full height. Those days were trying ones, to be sure. The birds were quiet at mid-day now, and the sun was hard at work from early to late. Indeed, the amount of heat he contrived to pour down upon that one Ear of Corn was something wonderful. It seemed almost as if he were fated to get a sunstroke, and take to having fits, or turn silly, as so many people do after being out in the sun. And those careless farmers had never thought to plant a tree, so as to shade him, nor even to buy a tent or marquee, as they call it, to protect his brains. Perhaps, after all, it was intended that he should harden, and whiten, and dry up in that fiery heat. Sometimes there would come a cloud across the sun, and then a nice refreshing thunder-shower came to put a little life into him. But if the rain lasted a moment too long, the farmer was sure to grumble. That was how things went when he was middle-aged, and the only event he had time to chronicle was the coming of a certain gipsy boy who lay down in the middle of the corn close by him, and lay there all night, crushing a great multitude of the wheat-ears, so that they were never able to hold up their heads again. But they had their revenge, for the moon shone out so that night, that the boy was moonstruck, and went away quite different to what he was when he came.

At last, as the Ear of Corn remembered,

Among the Corn,

came old age—white, reverend, beautiful old age, when all the growing, and changing, and ripening were over, and he had nothing to do but to wait for the harvest: What did it matter to him then if the sun scorched? It had done its worst for him, and could do no more. Was he not white, and heavy, and ripe—as full of grain, and as long of straw, and as perfect an ear altogether as you could wish? Now it was all over—the winter in the ground, the spring with its frosts, the summer with its burning heat: they had all ended in the ripeness and glory of autumn.

Then came the reapers and laid him low, there close by the Lark's nest, and the Poppy could not boast any more, and the Pimpernel had gone to sleep, and life was all over, with its fun and its suffering—its pleasure and its pain.

" It was all right, from beginning to

end," he said, thinking it over from the sheaf; "and if they liked to plant these grains again in the new ploughed earth, I could only wish it to come all over again— beginning, and middle, and end, for it has all turned out as it should do, and I've nothing at all to complain of."

XIII.

WHAT WILL TO-MORROW BRING?

IT was the first day of the Water-Lily's life, at least, the first day she had shown her round white face above the water, and opened her eyes to see all that was going on. And now the first day was coming to its end, and she was getting tired and sleepy with all the day's excitement.

"And yet I can't go to sleep yet," she sighed; "it is all so lovely and delicious, I can't think of going to sleep yet."

And so it was, very lovely and delicious indeed. In fact, I hardly know anything more delicious than that little bit of the river after the sun has set, when all the country is cool and still in the twilight. The water was so smooth all round the Lilies, and their own broad leaves looked so fresh and green. Then there were the tall whispering Poplars on the bank, throwing their shady reflections across the stream. And there was such a sweet smell of fresh-cut hay from the meadows, and all the tall Reeds, and Grasses, and Yellow Flags standing with their feet in the water, and looking refreshingly comfortable. And there were the arrow-shaped leaves under the bank, and the tall red flowers, as well as plenty of Forget-me-nots. Oh, those sentimental Forget-me-nots, I shall have fine tales to tell of them, if they don't take care!

Well, the Water-Lily was but a young thing as I told you, and like most young things she was fond of chattering. The elders of her family told her to be quiet and go to sleep, but she was busy counting up all the things she had seen in the day; and, you see, when you come to find everything new to you, it does take a good while to get over your surprise. In the morning early she had been looking at the sun for a long time, and couldn't make it out. Indeed, she stared at it so long that she might have gone blind altogether if it had not been for the afternoon shadows, which came just in time to save her. Then there were other strange things to look at—Birds, skimming Swallows that brushed their wings almost in her face, and the many-coloured, beautiful Kingfisher, who picked up his supper of a tiny bright Fish from under her very leaves; and there was the great clumsy Cow, who cooled her legs in the shallow stream, and dreamily looked down upon her with quiet admiration in her sleepy eyes, as the Water-Lily thought. Yes, there were many strange things that she had seen in the day, and little round Lily counted them over on her petals. "And what will to-morrow bring?" she wondered softly.

"Something more than to-day has brought, let us hope," murmured a large yellow Lily at her side, his petals were getting wrinkled and old-looking, and he spoke fretfully; "why, if we had many such days as this, I should die of the mopes. But I have seen something in my day, I have."

Our little friend would have turned her head to listen if she had been able, but flowers can't do that. They may talk to each other in their own quiet way, in prettier "flower-language" than you would ever find in those little, square, gilt-leaved

THE WATER-LILY.

books; but when they listen they don't move about, or they would let out the secret at once, and all the world would know of their conversations.

"I have seen something in my day," he went on, and all the sleepy Lilies roused up to listen. And then he began to talk about "long ago"—I dare say it seemed "long ago" to him if it was only a few days, because, you see, flowers have such short lives that they have to make the most of every minute.

"A long time ago," he said, "just about this time of day, I was enjoying myself in the breeze, and the dew was moistening my face quite pleasantly. I remember, I was thinking about the little Fishes that were skimming in and out around my stem, and tickling me with their fins, and I was laughing to myself to think of the Kingfisher on the

look-out for them.   But just then I saw a
little human boy come down to the bank—I
can see the bank from where I stand—and I
soon saw that he wanted to steal some of us.
And I laughed at him, for I knew he could
not reach me.   He stretched out a long stick
and caught me by the neck, but I slipped
away again as easily as possible.   He was quite
a little fellow, as those humans go, and
could not take care of himself.   He climbed
up that tree overhead at last, and tried to
reach me that way.   And then he came splash
into the midst of us, and half-a-dozen of my
friends went down with him to the bottom,
and I have not seen them since.   That is the
reason of the space in our midst to this day.
There was a great bubbling all round me,
and I felt myself seriously shaken, but I was
safe for all that, and I stood and waited.
By-and-by he came up again, and we stood

round and watched him, our yellow faces, and white faces, and our beautiful green leaves were all round him, and his hair lay all in the midst of us.   His was a pretty face, as human faces go, though it had not the roundness nor the cup-like beauty of a Lily; yet I think if they had left him there, he would hardly have spoilt our picture, would he ?

" But we were not to be quiet that evening. I was getting composed again after the shock, and thinking of a night's repose, when there came a great oar, cutting into our very midst, and the side of a boat pushed me half under the water.   Oh, it was wholesale destruction of us !   Lily after Lily bent its head, and broke its stem, and died ; or was caught and twisted and strangled round that cruel oar.   And when they lifted the child out, they never took any trouble to disentangle the poor flowers he

9

was clutching in his hand. Again they splashed and dashed through the water, and then they left us.

"It was like a battle-field that night, what with the torn leaves, the poor murdered blossoms, the terrible blanks in our family. I could not wonder—indeed, I could not wonder that my friend, the bat, passed backwards and forwards above us, uttering a shrill shriek of lamentation. And as for the white, ghost-like moths, they clustered and hovered around us, as if they would remind us of our vanished friends. Ah, my dear, you may well say, 'What will to-morrow bring?' There is no saying what may be the fate of a poor Water-Lily."

And all the Lily-buds wagged their heads in the evening breeze in meek assent. But most of them were asleep, dreaming of a very different kind of to-morrow, and laugh-

ing in their slumbers at the thought of all
the sweet sunshine, and all the light summer
air, and all the glad, buzzing, merry humming, and music of their bright, happy life.
And what did to-morrow bring? Why, it
brought the many-coloured Butterflies to pay
their morning-calls, and it brought the Bees
to whisper secrets in their ears and take pay-
ment in honey, and it brought all sorts of fun
and pleasure to the happy Water-Lilies.

XIV

THE WHITE CAMELLIA.

She was a beauty, and she came of a family of beauties, but she was the most beautiful of them all. She had been brought up with the greatest care, in the most carefully managed hot-house in the land. Every draught of air that could hurt her, every insect that could tease her, every ray of sun that could burn her, every little accident that could possibly befall her—her anxious gardener foresaw and provided against. And she repaid his care, for she was the very most beautiful flower of the whole season. From her earliest hour of budding they had watched for the precise minute of her most perfect bloom, and now it was close at hand. All the flowers that surrounded her wondered what happy fate was prepared for her, but I think they felt a thrill of excitement when they heard it at last.

"Yes, she will do, I thought she would," said the gardener, "she shall be the central flower in the Queen's bouquet to-night."

My dears, you will not wonder at the flowers' excitement. Going to court—why, it is nothing to it! Those people who dress up in thousands of pounds' worth of clothes just to kiss the Queen's hand, why, after all, they have but five minutes' pleasure at the most. But our beautiful Camellia, without any expense or any decoration, might go and look straight up into the Queen's face for ever so long. I was going to say without any trouble; but that would have been

hardly right, perhaps. There was a great
deal to go through first. There was the
shock of the gardening scissors or knife, I
forget which; and the sudden stoppage of
the sap, making her turn rather faint. But
that sap was precious, it was the finest, most
aristocratic in the land; and you find, as you
grow older, that people think a great deal
of having good sap in their veins. So the
clever gardener bound up the wound, as
only clever gardeners know how, binding it
round with fine wire, and let not a drop be
lost.

And then came the question of com-
panionship. It might have been a little
unpleasant to be crowded so close, and
pressed upon by those to whom the fair lady
had hardly been wont to speak at other
times. But, at any rate, it was a discomfort
that others besides the Camellia would have

that night, and to win far less favoured a
station than was hers unasked. Moreover,
she was very humble and unassuming, and
like the lady whose hand was to be her
place, she had none of that false pride that
disdains to notice its inferiors. Of course,
that was the supreme moment of her existence, when the royal eyes met her own, and
there were many among the flowers who
longed to know the sensation it gave her.
But, unlike some people I know who have
friends at court, they had not a scrap of such
tittle-tattle to repeat. I have no doubt the
sap bounded fast up and down the little way
it had to go, and there was great trembling
in the nervous fibres of the fair, white
petals.

By-and-by the hall was reached, the
greatest hall in London, the wonderful scene
of many a happy flower's night of gaiety.

And that night every flower's eye was strained to look at the royal box, and to penetrate through all obstacles to the Queen of the Fair, the beautiful, the unsurpassed, the far-famed Camellia.

There were unfortunates, there always are, whose position was such that they could get no sight. That feverish Geranium, for instance, in the Lady Mayoress' hair was so awkwardly placed that, fret and fume as she might, she couldn't catch one peep, though she could nearly have torn the lady's chignon off in her agony to make her turn her head.

"To have to go home and confess that you had *not* seen the Camellia that everybody was talking about—why, it was enough to kill you half-an-hour before your time!"

But flowers have their knowing little

ways as well as men.   Long before anything
was known of electricity by us, they had a
regular system of telegraphic communication
for such occasions as these, needing no ugly
posts, no wires, no readers, no message-boys to
spoil all.   Of course, it is expensive, but Lady
Flora's government has not learned to stint.
So messages passed backwards and forwards
from the Ferns in the royal box to the Ferns
under the orchestra, and alighted on diverse
head-dresses and bouquets on their way.
The only awkwardness was caused by that
one great crying evil, artificial flowers in the
hair.   It has been thought, since that notable
night, that there will be a strike in all the
gardens in England unless something is done
to put down this nuisance, so greatly dis-
gusted are the living, breathing, sensitive
creatures at the base attempts made to imitate
their beauty.   And I don't wonder, do you?

But I must not get in a rage, but go on to tell you quietly about the telegraphic performances of that night. At first they were all on the one subject, pithy and telling, as telegrams always are.

Orchestra Ferns : " How does she look ? "

Royal Box Ferns : " Fair as the moon."

O. Ferns: " Not abashed, not nervous ? "

R. B. Ferns : " Never a whit."

O. Ferns : " Making a sensation ? "

R. B. Ferns : " Admired by the Prince."

O. Ferns : " What now ? "

R. B. Ferns : " A smile from the Queen."

But this message was so eagerly caught at by all the fair ones on its way, that it was nearly lost in chignons and invisible nets, and was more than five seconds before it reached the orchestra. And in consequence of this there was a long pause, and when the electricity began to work again, it was about more common-place matters.

R. B. Ferns: "Hot down there?"

O. Ferns: "Terribly noisy."

R. B. Ferns: "Who is in Leslie's button-hole?"

O. Ferns: "Young Gloire de Dijon, nipped in his babyhood."   ·

R. B. Ferns: "Sign of the times."

O. Ferns: "Ah!"

An inaudible sigh through the hall, from hands, and heads, and button-holes.

R. B. Ferns: "How about sweet Maiden-hair?"

O. Ferns: "Headache from noise."

R. B. Ferns: "Better chance than we have."

O. Ferns: "Eh? you will outlive to-night!"

R. B. Ferns: "Don't know, heat tells."

O. Ferns: "Hard fate, yours!"

R. B. Ferns: "Hard, indeed!"

And there was another sympathetic sigh.

All the picked flowers envied the orchestra plants, happy and healthy in their several pots, even if the heat and noise did try them somewhat. But there, we must pay for pleasure, and it is rather a grand thing among the flowers not to outlive one night. There are less aristocratic bouquets or hair-flowers who are expected to appear twice in public. Ah, and there are bouquets so humble in their position in society that they get carefully preserved in water after their hour of gaiety.

But it is "the thing," and shows that

you serve a high and noble mistress, if you are thrown aside to die after the very first brief appearance. And we pay dearly to be aristocratic, if not happy.

XV

WISHING.

"Then, when evening comes,
Foxgloves ring their bells,
Calling all the sprites
From their distant cells."

YES, of course, that was their proper work, and generally they did it well enough, but one night they didn't. There was a dead silence through the woody hill-side, and the Moss, with its fairy cups, and all the Ivy and folks began to think that they should miss their evening company. It was very dull.

At last, just by way of a hint, a little

branch of tender Ivy that had been busy all
day climbing up an Oak-tree, began to hum
to itself—

"Those evening bells, those evening bells,"

but an angry Foxglove broke in fiercely—

" Do hold your tongue there ! as if that
wasn't the most tiresome song that was ever
sung."

Which is true, but he needn't have
said it.

The little soft Ivy was quite frightened,
and clung more tightly than ever to its great,
strong friend.

" My dear Foxglove, what is the matter ?" remonstrated a broad, honest Dock-
plant close by, as it received a little, hopping
Frog under its shelter—a little Frog that
had come to do some shy wooing, " whether
his mother would let him or no."

"It's nothing," growled the Foxglove, but he knew he was telling a story, so he added, quickly, "at least, it's nothing more to me than the others."

"Well, what is the matter with all of you?" asked a grandfather Dock, "you seem all in a dolorous state."

"It's only that I want"—began one, and all the other Foxgloves hastened to add, "and so do I," "and so do I."

"Well, come, what is it you all want?" asked the good grandfather, "anything that I can do for you?"

"Well, I don't suppose you can"—"I should not think you could; but there's no saying"—"Oh, I'm sure he can't!" cried all the Foxgloves, one after another.

"But let us hear, at all events," said the good-natured Dock.

"Well, we were wishing, we were all

wishing, we have been all day," began the tallest Foxglove, and then he hesitated, "that —that—that we could come out at the same time as the Primroses, and Anemones, and Wood-Sorrel."

"Well, I do declare!" shouted a merry, tall Thistle; "if wishes were horses, beggars would ride," and he shook backwards and forwards for very merriment.

"Crying for the moon to play with," remarked the Brake Fern, drily.

"Why, now, you needn't laugh at us, at any rate," retorted the Foxglove, "for it was your very own self that told us how much brighter and prettier the wood looked when first you peeped above ground and saw it all covered with white and yellow stars," and the poor fellow nearly cried to think of it.

"Of course, it did look prettier," answered the Fern, "but it was not meant for you, so

you should not grumble. People who do
not open their eyes until they have been
above ground ever so long, cannot expect to
see so much as people like me who see out of
every pore!"

"Oh, it is not true!" cried the Foxglove, quivering all over from the irritation
of these dry pompous words. "I don't see
why you should see a bit more than I do,
and it isn't my fault that I don't open my
eyes sooner."

"No, my little fellow," said the broad
Dock, kindly, "and it is none of your doing
either that you do not come out in the early
spring. And if you come to think of it,
there are nice things you would never see if
you did!"

"What?" asked the Foxglove, shortly;
he was choking back the anger.

"Why, my little fellow," went on the

Dock, "you would not see half such beautiful Heath, nor watch the Blackberries getting ripe, nor be able to smell the sweet Dog-Rose, and the Meadow-Sweet down in the ditch there."

"But the birds sing their sweetest in the spring, and the sun is not so hot, nor the ground so dry and hard."

"Yet you have a longer life than the frail spring flowers. They are over and gone ever so quickly, and then we all wait and watch for the stronger tints of the summer flowers, and are ever so pleased when your evening bells ring over the hill."

"But they are a great deal more tender and soft, the delicate stars and the white Wood-Sorrel, I know," murmured the Foxglove, not much soothed by his kind words.

"Well, if they are soft and tender, you

are strong and ruddy. Everything in its
place and its time. And do you know, I
fancy there is a change coming for you. It
will do you good, perhaps. Only ring
out your bells now, and let us have a
pleasant evening together, in case it is the
last."

"A change coming! A change for us!
Oh, dear!" and the red fellows were all
excited in a moment, and rang their bells with
all their might.

And I dare say the little fairies came
skipping, tripping, and dancing to have
their supper and their romps among the
flowers; or else they didn't. I really don't
know.

But, at any rate, to-morrow morning
came, and with it, ever so early, a schoolboy
through the wood. He had seen the tall
red Foxgloves last night, and had made up

THE FOXGLOVES.

his mind to fetch some for his little sick sister at home.

"I'll be up and get them before school, a whole jugful of them," he had said, and the Dock had heard him.

So he gathered away, pulling them up fiercely, and filling his arms, and the tall Thistle looked on and wondered who would ring the bells to-night. And the little soft Ivy was frightened, and clung close to her friend.

"Where are we going?" asked the Fox-gloves of each other; "Good-bye, pretty wood," they added, not quite sure if they were glad or sorry.

And before they had time to get thirsty, or to miss the sweet moisture of their own native soil, they found themselves all spread out on a bed in a cottage on the top of the hill, and two little, thin hands fitting them into a large blue jug. I think the strong flowers seemed to look down with a kind of pity on the pale, small face that was getting so eager over them.

"Mother, I wish I could go to the woods," said a weak voice from the midst of them, "but it's no use wishing, and Jem's good for bringing the flowers. Mother, he brought me the Primroses and the Buttercups long ago, and now they are over he brings me these."

"Ay, ay, my lamb, and he'll bring thee more when they're over."

"Yes, mother, I'm glad they don't come out all at once. What'll the next be, mother?"

"I don't know, my bairn; make the most of these, they'll be nigh about the last of the summer, I'm thinking. But they last a bit, the Foxgloves."

"Yes, mother. Oh, mother, I like them

so! they smell all of the woods and the heath, mother."

There was a little pause in the sick child's prattle. Could the flowers understand it? They did not make any answer, except to each other, at all events, and I didn't hear even that. But, perhaps, they were thinking.

" Mother, I'm very tired," the child said in the evening, " but I like to look at the flowers. Mother, I'm glad they didn't wait till next spring to come out, because I may not ever see the spring flowers again. I'm glad they're autumn flowers, mother."

And then the sick child went to sleep, and the setting-sun shone in at the cottage window. The Foxgloves looked out, for the jug was on the window-sill, looked out over the hill-side beneath them. Their brothers were ringing their bells for the sprites, but

from the cottage window I fancied I heard
a low murmur—

"We were wishing last night, we were
all of us wishing, but now last night is gone,
and to-day it makes all the difference!"

They did not say what made all the difference, but I thought I could guess.

XVI

GOING FARTHER, FARING WORSE.

"So the change is not quite so pleasant as you thought it would be?"

"Pleasant! Why, the change is murder to me!"

You would have been surprised if you had seen the two speakers of these very strong words. Indeed, *you* would never have heard the words at all. They were whispered in such tiny whispers on the breath of the Sweetbriar, and the White, Pink, and Moss Roses. But I heard them, because my hearing is very keen to the voice of the wee, wee flowers; and those dear little Ferns, those soft, green, tender things; oh, it was sweet to listen to their gentle whisperings.

It was the tiny Oak-fern that was panting out its lamentation. Let me show you the home he had come from, and then you will understand the change.

Far away, far away, in a wild, out-of-the way place, where, hundreds of years ago, the miners had dug down deep to look for iron and coal, and then had given up and left all the great holes to be overgrown again by the Ivy and creepers, there, down in the dark, the little fellow was born. If you went to visit that home now, you would cry out with delight as you peeped out from between the overhanging red rocks, up through the green boughs and waving trees crossing each other, and twisting their arms in and out to make a sweet sunshiny shade. And you

would say that it must be the greatest fun
in the world to clamber up and down those
steep rocks, squeezing yourself through the
narrow passages, and letting yourself down
into the deep holes.   But I think if I had
offered to leave you there for a whole night,
you would have looked up frightened, and said,
" Oh, please, don't ! "

It might be all very romantic and wild
to be down in that deep, deep shadow,
with, perhaps, just a moonbeam or two to
peep through the Beech-boughs, and the
owls shouting out to each other, in their
own noisy way, through the wood, and the
little birds awaking with a half-frightened,
sleepy cry as they heard them—it might be
all very romantic, but it gives one a shudder
to think of it, all the same.

Well, I don't think our little friend,
Master Oak-fern, was nervous or timid about

these long nights. He was quite used to it, you see. It was not anything to him if the trees rustled overhead, all in the silence; he knew it was only a fox going out "in a hungry plight," or a rabbit that had bad dreams and was taking the night-air to refresh himself. No, it was not the nights that troubled him. What he did long for, and what he often stretched his neck to reach, was a little sunshine. So dark it was in the shadow of his great rock, and so cold too, and damp. What if some day he should get the rheumatism, living so long in that damp, red clay?

And there were little Ferns—he could see them when he stretched out to the utmost—whose place was all up in the sunshine on the very tip-top of the rock. Ah, little Oak-fern, little Oak-fern, what if the damp earth and the cool shadow are just the things needed to keep you fresh, and green, and healthy?

But then it was so dull down in the hollow, the very commonest Brake had a better chance of seeing life than our poor little fellow. The very owls avoided the damp, lower rocks; and as for the merry rabbits, and the little mice, and the bright woodpeckers, why they never dreamed of such low, chilly places. Nothing but the cold creeping lizards, and creatures of that sort, ever came near him.

"I am quite out of the world," sighed the little Oak-fern, "I had as soon not live as live like this."

He quite forgot that out of sight is out of danger, and that his very solitude saved him from being gobbled up by the merry wood creatures, who make no more of eating a beautiful Fern than you do of eating parsley and butter.

" I had rather go farther, even if it is to fare worse," he thought—just as we do sometimes in our bold discontent, forgetting that there is a kind, loving Wisdom who chooses the right place for the little Fern, and the right place for you and me also.

Well, the day came at last that was to lift the little fellow out of his damp hollow, and to make a great change for him altogether. A great, strong, iron scoop came under his roots, disentangling them all from the stiff clay, and lifting him bodily out of the ground. Then he was laid carefully in a basket with some Hart's-tongues, a Spleenwort or two, and three Shield-ferns, and while he was quivering all over, and all his sap seemed in a wild fever of excitement, he heard children's voices praising him and exulting over him.

And so, by-and-by, he hardly knew how,

THE FERN.

he was in a new home, all among rocks and
sands, and all kinds of strange relatives of his
own, with the bright sun streaming down
on him, and the sweet breath of Roses and
Carnations floating all over him.   They gave
him plenty of fresh water to drink, and
very soon he was as merry and talkative as
possible.

Close beside him was a lusty young
Brake, and when the night fell on them, all
dark and still, the two Ferns began their
whispered confidence.   Master Brake had
been for some time on this " fernery," as he
called it, and he seemed to be having " a good
time," as the Yankees say.   He could remember his life in the Park, but he did not care
to think of it.   He had been just in the
middle of one of those wild, hilly places
where the happy Ferns grow all round the
trunks of the old Oak-trees, mixed up with

Heath, and Moss, and dry Grass, and send-
ing out the strong, pleasant smell that makes
one think of picnics, and blackberries, and
nutting days, and sun-burnt faces, and all that
sort of fun.

But then, you see, perhaps the Ferns
don't get quite the best part of it all. In
their baby-days they like to keep their little,
soft fingers all doubled up tight, and rough
human hands will sometimes persist in pulling them open, and so very likely breaking
off a great many of them. And when they
are grown up tall and strong, those same
human hands will often cruelly pull them
up on purpose to cut open their hearts to see
the picture of Prince Charlie in the Oak-
tree, which is a picture that the gallant, loyal
Brake would far rather hide away in his
inmost soul. And then there are all those
other dangers, the wild republican rabbits,

who burrow at the roots of everything to make their lawless colony, and there is no knowing what a rabbit may nibble when he comes scampering out of his horrid hole. And there are the pheasants ready to sit down and hatch a little family on your very face, and then attract a great, heavy-booted huntsman, with his gun and his sniffing dogs, to come and trample you down in all directions.

"Oh, there's no doubt about it," said the Brake, "a good fernery, well taken care of, is the place for a free, happy life."

Nor, strange to say, did he change his mind as the days went on. Our more delicate little Oak-fern soon began to see that, as the Conservatives say, all change is not gain. The sun beat so terribly on his little, tender frame, and there was no shady rock here. The soil was so dry and sandy that he thought longingly of the damp clay he had once scorned. But it was when, at last, the daily supply from the watering-pot ceased, and parched, and faint, and weary beyond description, he drooped his faded fronds on the hot stone beside him—it was then that he gave that despairing answer to the sturdy Brake at his side.

Then I listened, listened very closely, for I was half afraid that there would come some harsh, unsympathizing answer from the stronger, less sensitive Fern. But it was not so; perhaps the Brake had learned a lesson from that human way of prying into his brothers' hearts, for he was very gentle, and never said one careless word. But it seemed to me — it may have been fancy — but it seemed to me that he stooped his broad self so as to cast some little shadow over his prostrate friend. It was a very small kindness, and perhaps it was the evening breeze that helped him to do it, but he certainly did contrive just a little to shelter the poor little fellow.

And I thought I caught a cheery whisper about a nice rainy cloud coming up from the west.   At any rate, he did not turn away to laugh with the great, strong Hart's-tongue over the delicacy of some folks and their habit of fainting.   He just waited and watched.

And, by-and-by, there was a rumbling in the distance, and then a bright flash, and, though the Oak-fern was too ill to know it, the sun's hot face was quite covered up, and very soon large, cool drops were falling. And then, didn't it pelt?

Of course, I had to scamper into the house as fast as a rabbit.   When it was all over, I went out again, and wasn't it pretty   to   see   the   little   Oak-fern   all

upright again, looking up at its tall friend
and whispering—

" I should like to go home, but it's nice
here, too, now it is.   And I think we are
taken care of everywhere, I do!"

XVII.

YOUNG MAC.

I REALLY must tell you about young Mac's marvellous and extraordinary rescue from a painful and shameful death.

Now, I wonder what your lively imagination has done with those three lines. Perhaps you have made a pretty picture to yourself of a yellow-haired Scotch boy hanging by a yard of twine over a precipice.

Oh, you little goose! Young Mac was no Scotch boy, nor Irish boy either; he was neither more nor less than a sleek, slender, handsome fish of the fairest proportions and the finest mottled tints. When he is grown up, perhaps it may be right to call him John Mackerel, Esq., but at present we may speak of him as his schoolfellows, the little Soles, and Plaices, and Herrings do, and call him plain Mac.

Can you guess what a beautiful playground young Mac and his friends had to play in? I have often looked down at it from the top of the high red cliffs, and half envied the happy little fellows. For on a glaring hot, scorching day in August what can be so delicious as that clear, soft stretch of sea? You can look right into it, and see how cool and sleepy it seems as it lazily splashes the green rock, or rocks the little pebbles backwards and forwards, they laughing softly all the time.

That was where young Mac lived with all his brothers and sisters, and fine fun they had of it. Such races and chases as they had. There were given courses marked out on their playground by little sea-weedy rocks, and young Mac won every race. And, of course, this was more fun to him than all the Regattas or Light Blue and Dark Blue races in the world.

And then to play at hide-and-seek among those bunches of Sea-weed and all among the Shells, could there ever be better fun than that? Only fancy, just for one minute, all the glorious adventures of hiding away in those snug dark corners, knocking up against the Crabs and Lobsters, tumbling into the middle of the Jelly-fishes, or thumping up against the red Anemones, or the pointed Limpets.

Somebody wrote a whole book the other day about " Putting yourself in his place," but I am sure if you only put yourself in young Mac's place, you wouldn't wish to get out of it again.

Therefore, in case you should be very anxious to turn into a fish, which would be a wish not easily to be gratified, I will tell of young Mac's troubles as well as his pleasures.

It was just the beautiful evening-time, when the grand old sea was getting grey in the twilight. All the little Macs were very lively, for this was the time of day when they liked to see the upper world. The sun was too strong for their fishy eyes in the daytime, but now they could look about quite well. And each in turn gave a jump high into the air, and had a peep at the high red cliffs, and the pebbly beach far off, and at the little boats dotted about all round them, and at the great blue sky, with stars just peeping out, above them. For some time young Mac and his brothers were

UNDER THE WAVES.

alone in their play; but by-and-by there came sweeping along a great crowd of fathers, and mothers, and uncles, and aunts, and cousins, and young Mac found himself hurrying along in the midst of them all. I wonder why it was that old Master Smith, on the top of the cliff, who had been watching the little fellows at their play, lying quietly on his chest on the grass, now suddenly jumped up and began to wave his arms! And I wonder why it was that all those little boats, so idle and quiet a few minutes before, were all of a sudden so busy!

Young Mac swam along eagerly enough, thinking it all great fun, until, to his amazement, he found himself caught up by some strange net-work, and together with all his friends whisked straight into a little boat.

Gasping, and panting, and frightened they lay all in a heap, while the busy sailors laughed to think how many fine fish they had caught.

And now, can you put yourself in young Mac's place? You would be puzzled to guess how it feels to be out of water when one is accustomed to be in it. Can you fancy the dry heat of his poor shining skin, the panting, stifling suffocation, the gasping for water, the writhing, fainting, sick feeling? Poor Mac! poor Mac! he gave it up at last, and lay quite still, his tail on his aunt, and his head on his second cousin, and made up his mind to die. Ah! the sweet sound of splashing oar, the sweet, sweet murmur of his own native sea, but his senses were growing dull, very soon it would be all still for him!

Well, they rowed on, and they rowed on, till the boat grated on the shingle, and then they began to shovel out the fish by handfuls into large baskets. In a little while the men and women would be crying, " Fine Mackerel, fine live Mackerel," all about the streets. Would they be really *live* Mackerel, or dying Mackerel, or dead Mackerel. Our poor young Mac was certainly only half conscious of the rough hands that threw him back into the dear cool sea, or of the rough voice that said—

"Why, he's such a little 'un, we'll give him another chance!"

XVIII

LITTLE NEDDY.

ONLY a little Donkey! Just one of those creatures that little boys with no sense think they may kick and beat just as they like. Of course, such very small boys would not care to read about Neddy, so this chapter is meant for people more manly and less silly.

Little Neddy! ah, in his baby days he was such a sweet little fellow, I don't believe anybody could have hurt him. He used to look up at you, with his little innocent face, as he stood by his mother's side on the common, all among the yellow gorse and the purple heath, and he would let you pat him or stroke him, just as you liked. Yes, one would have thought that there could not be anybody in the world quite cruel enough to hurt little Neddy. But, then, those small boys! Ah, there's no knowing!

Anyhow, this is what came about.

A number of these very small folks— small, I mean, in sense, and heart, and all that, they were lanky enough in arms and legs — well, a number of these came up from the beach, where they had been teazing the crabs, and the shrimps, and the jelly-fish.

I suppose they had got into a fit of teazing, and didn't know where to stop. So they began to pull little Neddy's ears and tail, and to stick thorns into him, until he could stand it no longer, but had to run away. And then they ran after him — wretched small boys ! — down the lane, into the high-road, and all along between the hedges, across the green, and through the village, and past the church. But little Neddy ran too fast for them, so they were tired out, and had to give it up.

But the poor little fellow was tired, too, and he lay down on the grass, his heart beating ever so fast. He was all alone, and he could not find his way back to his mother. Indeed, before night came on he was a poor little prisoner in the village-pound. This was the saddest part of little Neddy's baby-life, and I think you can guess his feelings. He was very lonely, and he soon grew very hungry, and he was terribly mammy-sick. How was he to be sure that he should not be left to die there ?

However, just before morning came—when it was very dark indeed — there came two gipsy-men up to the pound. They came very quietly, and I am afraid, they were really something very like thieves. They climbed over the old stone wall, and then, with ropes and other things, they lifted Neddy right out into the road. They spoke very gently and kindly to him, for they did not want him to make a noise; and then they lifted him into a little cart, and drove away with him.

When breakfast-time came, our young friend found himself tied to a post close to a large gipsy camp, with plenty of grass to eat, and an old Mother Donkey not far off. It was not his mother,

—*she* was ever so far away—but Neddy soon grew fond of her, and, I think, almost forgot his old baby-life on the common.

This was how Neddy's gipsy-life began. They were naughty people that had stolen him, and they often gave him hard blows and bad words. Yet he had his friends among them, too, black - eyed children who loved the little stranger donkey, and liked to feed and pet him. They would put flowers round his neck and give him their own breakfast to eat, calling him all kinds of loving names.

One little fellow, with blacker eyes, and browner skin, and whiter teeth than all the rest, was Neddy's namesake. The rough men called them " The two Neddies," and they treated them equally to kicks and cuffs. And whenever they were particularly badly used, they always sought comfort in each other.

How fond they were of each other! Together they trotted along the dusty roads, together they lay down to rest at hot mid-day, and together they had their supper in the moonlight. When little boy Neddy got a beating he would cry out his troubles with his arm round his friend's neck, and if little donkey Neddy got a beating, he was sure of loving sympathy from the same brown arm and the same tearful voice.

Towards the end of the summer, while it was still very hot, the little brown gipsy-boy was taken very ill. He was in such dreadful pain that they thought he would die, and even his rough father got frightened, and sent for the doctor. And when the doctor came, what do you think he saw? He had to creep under the low, round tent, and look about in the dark before he saw the sick child. And then he caught sight of a little, burning, feverish face, with very bright eyes and rough black head lying on a very strange pillow, the shaggy side of a young donkey!

You can fancy what he said at once, but the little plaintive voice, and the eager, pitiful eyes touched him, as the child pleaded—

" Oh, don't take Neddy away! He loves me, nobody else does!"

"No, no, we won't take Neddy away," said the kind doctor, " he will keep you warm, and, perhaps, help to cure you."

But I do not think he thought there was much chance for the child, for he looked very grave as he talked to the rough, noisy father.

And, indeed the little fellow got worse and worse, but still he clung tighter and tighter to his strange friend. Had not the doctor told him that Neddy would keep him warm, and wasn't he getting cold, very cold!

And so the hours went on, and by-and-by they found that the bright eyes were shut, and the little fellow had fallen asleep on his strange pillow.

Next · time the Doctor came he did not look quite so grave, and the time after he did not look grave at all, but said that his little patient would certainly get well again.

And so he did. And after that, as you will fancy, he was fonder than ever of his shaggy pillow.

So the two little Neddies went trotting about the country once more, and where they are now, I am sure I don't know.

THE END.

Simmons & Botten, Printers, Shoe Lane, E.C.

www.ingramcontent.com/pod-product-compliance
Lightning Source LLC
Chambersburg PA
CBHW020618030726
47497CB00007B/2306